SAY YOU'1

RECLAIMING HEAVEN BOOK 2

E.R. WHYTE

Say You'll Be Mine
Copyright © 2020 by E.R. Whyte
All rights reserved.

This novel is entirely a work of fiction. The names, characters, and incidents portrayed in it are the work of the author's imagination. Any resemblance to actual persons, living or dead, events or localities is entirely coincidental.

ALSO BY THE AUTHOR

As **E.R. WHYTE**
Contemporary Romantic Suspense
And New Adult/College

RECLAIMING HEAVEN DUET
Say You Love Me
Say You'll Be Mine

As **ELLE RAE WHYTE**
Contemporary Sweet Romance

ONLY IN OCRACOKE SERIES
Just a Crush
Just a Neighbor
Just a Friend

DEDICATION

For all of those "just one more page" late night readers.

Cheers to that cup of coffee in the morning, and never stop reading.

CONTENTS

Acknowledgments   i

Preface   3

Chapter 1   5

Chapter 2   13

Chapter 3   19

Chapter 4   32

Chapter 5   41

Chapter 6   48

Chapter 7   55

Chapter 8   66

Chapter 9   73

Chapter 10   79

Chapter 11   93

Chapter 12   99

Chapter 13   111

Chapter 14   120

Chapter 15   127

Chapter 16   135

Chapter 17   141

Chapter 18   148

Chapter 19   156

Chapter 20   164

Chapter 21   167

Chapter 22   175

Chapter 23   181

Chapter 24   185

Chapter 25   195

Chapter 26   204

Chapter 27   210

Chapter 28   221

Chapter 29   224

Chapter 30   230

Chapter 31   241

Epilogue   245

ACKNOWLEDGMENTS

I couldn't have completed this work without the support and encouragement of friends, family, and most particularly author buddies. A published work has been a dream a lifetime in the making, and I will be forever thankful to those who believed in my ability to realize it.

Preface

IN ALL THESE WEEKS OF BEING TORMENTED BY THE SPECTER OF A STALKER, I hadn't thought much about the *when* of being taken. Such a scenario was an *if*, something to be wary of, to be prepared to defend myself against. It was a possibility, but one without form and shape.

I never allowed myself to acknowledge that possibility, to feed it the fuel of my fear and allow it to assume flesh and substance.

That was my first mistake.

My second: I'd clung to the *why*, and not the *who*. Why me? What had I done to attract this twisted attention? What could I do to make it stop?

I wish I'd pursued the *who* with more vigor. I wish I'd looked closer. Maybe then I wouldn't be here.

But what was that old saying? If wishes were horses, then beggars would ride.

1
Shiloh

IT'S BARELY LUNCH TIME WHEN I GET HOME BUT EXHAUSTION, the kind that derives from the sheer depletion of emotional reserves, weights every muscle as I push open the creaky front door.

As of this morning, I am no longer a teacher at Kennon High. A feeling like lead sits heavy in every muscle at my failure. My first real job—if I don't count the strip club—gone. I barely lasted two months.

The first thing I do after dumping my bag on the floor is crack open a bottle of the finest grocery store vintage I have in the fridge while I run a bath, knowing the combination of hot water and chilled wine will soothe my jangled nerves.

This has been a shit day. Right now, I resolve to do nothing more for the remainder of the day except get naked, get drunk, and get wet. Although not necessarily in that order. Shedding my clothes, I pile my hair on top of my head and look around for my robe. Not seeing it, I shrug. "Fuck it."

I'm in a *fuck it* kind of mood. If the bastard still has cameras on me he's going to get an eyeful. Sticking both middle fingers up, I do a little spin for good measure.

Strolling buck naked into the kitchen, I pour the wine into a glass and carry both it and the bottle back to the bathroom with me. Then I take a few gulps to get that party started and sink down into the tub with a sigh. The fragrance of lavender and citrus essential oils rises around me and I close my eyes.

As soon as the quiet settles around me thoughts of the morning trickle in. Jaw clenching, I remember the words on my classroom wall, the smell of the paint lingering in the air. Who would do this to me? Why? If the objective was to get me fired, I guess he won.

Up to this point, the person stalking me has been content to call and breathe, send me creepy text messages, and make certain I know he's there. Watching.

He's been more of a nuisance than anything to truly fear, an inconvenience interfering with my job and my peace of mind.

But this...his attack on my classroom, the show of aggression in the awful words painted in red on its walls...it scares me. He's angry. He wanted to hurt me.

Tears burn behind my eyes and thicken in my throat, but I stuff them back. I don't want to cry. Once I start, I know it'll be the kind of weeping that doesn't stop. I wouldn't let myself cry when my mom died, knowing that giving in to that weakness would undermine my ability to be strong. I didn't want Sammy to wake and find his sister a blubbering mess by his bedside. I wanted him, instead, to find me strong, capable—just like Mom. So many times since then, I've felt these tears prowling just beneath the surface, begging for release. Psychologically I understand they're a means of leeching emotional poisons from my soul. Emotionally, I don't think I'll survive the catharsis.

I don't understand why, of all people, the bastard picked me to obsess over. I'm nothing special. I'm not a celebrity. Not beautiful. Not rich. I don't even think I'm particularly interesting.

I scrunch my fingers around the edge of the tub and force my thoughts away from this morning and the fact that I no longer have a job. *Happy thoughts*, I think, instead. Whiskers on kittens, rain on a tin roof, and sunset over the ocean. *Gunner*.

It seems inevitable for my thoughts to turn to him in conjunction with happiness. Despite the fact that my connection to him is almost certainly part of the reason I have lost my position at the high school; he has made me smile more often in the past month than anything else. His humor, his steadfast nature, his protectiveness...all these things combine to make him more magnetic than any man I've known.

And then there's his physical appeal. No man has ever given me the feels like Gunner Ford does. It's a little scary. The brush of his eyes is a physical touch. His hands...they're electric. They give me chills; they make me burn. They make me clench and send me flying.

It's hard to believe that boy I kissed in a closet years ago...all nose and eyes and long, lean limbs...is this same man pushing me to give him a chance. Give *us* a chance.

Temptation is a physical presence when he's near, and I'm getting tired of fighting it. I feel like I've been fighting against being honest with my feelings so long. The constant lie I've been telling myself—that I don't care, that I don't want him—is exhausting.

Because I do.

At least a decade ago, I read one of my mother's romance novels. They were strictly forbidden to me, but that didn't stop me from plucking one at random from her shelf and hiding it in my bedroom.

I read it with the door locked, when I knew Mom was busy with something and wouldn't be checking on me any time soon. I don't remember much about the story, other than there was a Viking warrior and a captured maiden from a distant land. Thinking back, my thrilling to their story was probably my first indication that I'd never be a staunch feminist.

The Viking wrapped his captured maid in warm furs and cherished her—but only after she humbled herself to him, admitting she needed his strength, wanted his protection. Admitting she needed and wanted *him*.

When I read the kissing scenes, I took careful notes on the way their passion made me feel. The fluttering in my stomach. That tightness in my chest.

I knew, even then, that I wanted someone to make me feel that way. Someone who would demand nothing less than my complete capitulation.

It's the most bizarre set of circumstances I never could have imagined, but I think that someone is Gunner.

He makes me feel all the things. The butterflies. The spasm in my chest. The ever-present ball of need low in my gut.

It makes me wonder what kind of lover he is—not that I have anyone to compare him with. Is he a passionate, uninhibited lover, or an organized, methodical one? Tender and attentive? Alpha and demanding? Does he talk dirty, or do his work in focused silence?

I am getting turned on thinking about the possibilities. Intense and fast, against a wall, maybe. Hands all over the place. Or all engrossed concentration, one inch of flesh at a time, beginning with the top of my head and working his way down. Or maybe with my toes and working his way up.

The bath water sloshes as my legs move restlessly beneath its surface. Taking another deep gulp of my wine, I set it down on the floor with one hand and then the other hand to travel down the plane of my stomach to that pulsing ache between my legs.

I've touched myself before—I mean, honestly, who can get to the ripe old age of twenty-two without having masturbated? But I usually save it for night, when I'm tucked into bed and the lights are off. The bathroom is bright and distracting in its pragmatism, but I shut it out and play my hands down my skin anyway.

Parting my slick folds, I slide a finger inside myself, closing my eyes and letting my head fall back against the cold cast iron at my neck. I feel a spear of hot water trickle inside, a poor mimicry of what I'm craving.

Gunner's eyes glow against the back of my eyelids, steel and cotton clouds against a gray sky. I can almost feel him, if I try.

Gunner's lips against my throat, warm and dry.

Gunner's hands on my flesh, firm and resolute.

My back arches and I spread my legs wider in the close confines of the tub as I touch myself and think about the man I left behind, a whimper escaping my lips. He could be here with me now. All I have to do is call him. I work my fingers faster, more firmly, knowing all the while that it's not my fingers I want on my body.

There's a knot of expectancy coiling in my gut, spooling tighter and tighter as I stroke my way to completion. I'm close...so close...a silent cry on my lips.

My phone, positioned on the toilet beside the tub, buzzes with an incoming call. Eyes still closed, I jolt but ignore it.

Bzzz. Bzzz. The buzzing does not stop, an annoying insect intruding in my consciousness. Slitting one eye, I sit up enough to see Gunner's name on the display. *Gunner. The man himself.* I lever myself up and reach for the phone, the idea of getting myself off while I talk to him making me bite my lip. Should I tell him? Would he even know? *I'd better make sure he's not driving.*

The phone falls to the floor as I grab for it and I curse, my concentration completely blown. Grabbing my towel from the floor beside the tub, I dry my hands and reach for the phone, just in time to see a text message flash across my notifications. I scan it quickly, terror settling like lead in my belly and pushing away all remnants of desire.

Gunner: Shiloh. Pick up the phone baby your stocker fund with my truck I think he's trying to separate us

Gunner: I need to know you're okay

The words run together, some of them nonsense, and after a moment of confusion I recognize the use of talk-to-text. It doesn't matter what settings are used, talk to text does not work well with a southern accent. I manage to grasp that my stalker went after Gunner's truck, and fear chokes my throat. He wants to know if I'm okay? What about him? What happened with his truck? Did he wreck? If he's hurt…

The possibility of an accident sends my mind diving immediately to another accident, nearly two years ago. A collision with a trucker checking his texts send Sammy to extended critical care and my mother to her grave.

I'm switching to the phone app to call when another call comes through and I answer immediately.

"Gunner? Gunner, are you okay? What happened? What's going on?"

"It's just the truck. I'm fine. I'm headed your way, though. I don't trust this guy." The words are tense, and I can hear the rain coming down in sheets in the background. But he's talking. Driving. He's not injured.

Just like that, moisture floods my eyes. God, I was such a bitch to him earlier, in my classroom. My anger over what the stalker had done, how it had cost me my job…all of it had bubbled over in impotent rage, making me lash out at the one person who I knew had my back.

He had been trying to help me, trying to comfort me, and I was cold and cutting, shutting him out completely. I start to apologize but choke the words off. I'll do that in person, when I can look him in the eye.

My words are choked when I answer, shame mixed with my panic from a few minutes ago clogging my throat. "Okay."

There's a long beat of silence. In the background I can hear the rush of water pounding against the metal of the vehicle. Then his voice comes, hesitant. "Shiloh? Are you crying?"

"No! I thought you were hurt. I didn't want to answer my damn phone. Didn't want to talk to you, and then you said he had messed with your truck, and I-I'm so s-sorry." The day abruptly catches up with me, and although I try to stifle it, shove it back down into its pit, a sob bursts forth. Maybe I'm a little drunk.

"Shy, it's all right. You needed space. I get it."

But the fucking dam has burst now. *Fuck.* I hate to cry, and suddenly, I can't stop crying. I fight it, hiccupping into the hand I have clamped across my mouth. Even over the phone, I can sense Gunner's agitation, and I feel horrible. He just had his truck damaged over my crap. He doesn't need anymore.

"Okay, look, I'm sorry. You don't have to talk to me when I get there. Just…stop crying. I'm getting off the phone now, Shy. It's hard to see anything; the wipers aren't working right over the damage to the windshield. I'll be over in a little while, okay? Lock your doors for me?"

I try to pull it together, murmuring some kind of assent. *I am not a crybaby. Shiloh Anne Brookings Does Not Cry.*

"Good girl." With those parting words, dead air replaces the sounds of the call, and Gunner is gone.

2
Gunner

THE SCRAPE ON MY HEAD WON'T STOP BLEEDING. I wince as the nurse dabs at it, first with alcohol and then with cotton gauze.

"Sorry, dear," she coos in sympathy and holds up a needle. "I'm going to give you a little numbing agent, and the doctor will be by in just a few minutes to do your stitches. Ready? Little stick."

I nod and steel myself, focusing over her shoulder as she slides the needle into my forehead. Little stick, my ass. That shit hurts. I don't like needles. Not one bit.

Finished, she gathers the metal tray scattered with everything she needed to patch me up and walks briskly out of the room.

Alone at last. I poke an exploratory finger at the bruising beginning to mottle my ribs and hiss when pain blooms. Unbidden that old movie—Spaceballs, I think—springs to mind. *That's gonna leave a mark.*

I shake my head, mildly amused with myself. Already has, looks like.

Rapid-fire, memories of the accident hurtle back, making me nauseous. I close my eyes, willing them away. They remain, though. The sensation of weight, all around as gravity yanked on the chain that was my truck. The truck encapsulating me, alive with a thousand pinpricks of flying glass. The lash of rain through the shattered window and the groan of metal.

Held in place by the seatbelt, I was nonetheless a rag doll jerked this way and that as the truck tumbled ever downward.

And then came the stillness when the truck stopped. Stifling. Thick.

I'm not sure how long I sat crumpled over the steering wheel at the bottom of that ravine. It could have been minutes, or it may have been hours. When I awoke the rain was still pouring down, soaking through my clothes immediately and chilling me to the bone as I climbed dazedly from the cab.

After a few stumbles and slides of my boots in the mud, I started to trudge up the hill, then remembered my phone and backtracked. It was still plugged into its dashboard holder, intact, so I called for help before beginning the upward trek once again.

Fire and EMS met me when I was half-way up the hill, and a couple of them took over, half-carrying me to the top.

"Knock, knock. You decent?"

Nonna. I shake myself loose of the memories. "Come on in, Nonna."

I'm in a tiny, three-sided procedure room in our emergency department, a salmon-colored privacy curtain forming the fourth wall and door. I watch as Nonna pulls the curtain back a few inches and peeks in. Her face crumples. "Oh, *polpetto. Povero piccolo!*"

I stand, hiding my grimace as sore and strained muscles immediately protest. I felt okay until I tried to move; now, though, I can feel the lactic acid burn in every limb, I suppose from where I tensed and fought against the downward momentum. Nonna resorts to Italian when she's pissed or royally upset. "I'm fine, Nonna. Just a little banged up." I pull her into a hug, and notice Esme standing behind her. "Hey, kid."

"Hey, yourself. What happened, Gunner?" Without giving me a chance to answer, she rattles on. "Oh, I called Dad. I figured you already had but thought I would anyway. He said, and I quote, for us to "get our asses over here" and make sure you hadn't downplayed things." She eyes me critically. "Anything broken?"

When she pauses to breathe, I sit back down on the bed. "I'm perfectly fine, I swear it. Nothing broken except my pride. I swerved to miss a deer, and—"

"Your head is bleeding through that gauze. It's kind of gross."

"Doc's coming to stitch it up in a minute. Head injuries always bleed like a bitch. Sorry, Nonna."

"So, you hit a deer and decided to take a header into a ravine? Moron."

"I didn't hit the deer. I avoided it because I'm talented like that."

"Be better to hit the deer next time, I think. The tree's not as forgiving."

I ruffle her hair, messing it up. She swats at my hand and dips away from me, squealing, and Nonna takes a seat in the single guest chair along the wall, clucking.

"You stop. Not in here."

The doctor and another nurse step around the corner and into my cubicle, eyeing the crowded space.

"Es, take my phone and call Shiloh. Let her know what an idiot I am." I catch her eye meaningfully. "Downplay."

"Got it." Phone in hand, she disappears. She'll probably call Miles, too. She's always asking about him.

"Okay, Mister Ford. Ready for these stitches?" I nearly look around for my dad, but realize she's talking to me. Dad's in California, but I have no doubt he'll be back before morning. The doctor, a middle-aged woman with dark hair and tired eyes, steps beside me and prods at the gash on my forehead. "How's that feel?"

"How's what feel, ma'am?"

She shakes her head slightly. "You southern boys. That would be Doctor-Ma'am, please." She smiles to show she's teasing.

In a matter of moments, she has repeated the cleansing procedure and is stitching me with efficient movements. After a single wince, Nonna exits the room, presumably to wait with Esme.

"So, will I be okay to leave tonight, Doctor-Ma'am?"

"I don't think that will be a problem provided we have guardian permission and you have someone to stay with? I believe I was told your father is in California at the moment?"

"Yes, but it should be okay. I'm eighteen, and my grandmother has guardian status, as well."

"Okay. I'll want to observe you for a little while for that concussion, but I think you'll be good to go soon." Finished with her stitching, she places a few bandages over several other cuts that don't merit stitches, and palpates my ribs once again. "Okay, all good. Relax for a little while so we can continue to keep an eye on things. I'm going to have a nurse move you to a room so we have the procedure room free for emergencies. You can tell your family you'll be in..." She checks her tablet. "Room 427. And I'll have a nurse start working up your release paperwork."

Esme comes back in a few minutes later. "Shy is on the way."

"What? I didn't mean for you to—"

"Simmer down. She was already on the way. She knew you were here already, somehow." I groan, although a not-so-secret part of me revels in the proof that she cares. "When are they cutting you loose?"

"Not for a while. Doc wants to monitor my concussion for a while. Where's Nonna?"

"She nodded off in the waiting room."

"Why don't you guys leave? There's no point in you staying. I'm fine, and Shiloh's on the way. I'll get a ride with her."

Esme shrugs. "If that's what you want."

"I'd like Nonna to get to bed before too much later."

"Fair enough." She leans in and surprises me with a kiss on my cheek. "I'm glad you're okay, you weirdo."

"Thanks, dweeb. Love you."

She leaves, pulling the curtain closed behind her, and within seconds the room is a silent bubble, cocooned within the noise of the emergency department. I lay back on the bed and rest my hands on my stomach, staring up at the fluorescent light in the ceiling.

Shiloh's going to kill me. Worse, she's probably going to cry, given how emotional she was earlier.

I'm pissed at myself for getting in the accident to begin with. Granted, there were extenuating circumstances with the rain and the windshield damage, but I shouldn't have driven the truck in the first place.

Shiloh is so skittish as it is. I wish I hadn't told her that her stalker messed with my truck. It wasn't anything she needed to know and it's going to freak her out.

Worse, it'll likely fuel her resistance to being with me—as if she needed one more reason.

Every muscle in my body aches viciously, but I push the discomfort away. Instead, I sit up and draw my shirt over my head.

At least she won't be able to see those marks.

Sitting back, I close my eyes and wait.

3
Shiloh

AFTER GUNNER'S CALL, I dress simply in a pair of sweats and a ratty tee-shirt that proclaims, 'real cameras don't text' and sit on the couch. Needing something to occupy my hands until Gunner arrives, I pick up my knitting and set the wine on the table in front of me, feeling inexplicably nervous.

Countless rows of yarn later, I check the time on my phone. It has been almost an hour since Gunner called. Surely that was enough time for him to get here, even if he'd had to make a stop. I almost wish I had a dog or something to curl up with and take my mind off of things. Maybe I'll look into that when Sammy comes home, take him and pick one out together at the humane society. But for now...I should call or text?

I'm not sure of the rules. Not sure if there are rules, or boundaries we shouldn't cross. I haven't dated in literal years, and that was a fiasco. Before a month had passed, Shane had turned to someone else to give him what he needed in a girlfriend.

When did I become this girl? I wondered. I went from being pissed that I'd lost my job to exhibiting signs of a stage five clinger. And with one of my little brother's friends, no less. In the eyes of most people, a kid.

And are we dating? I'm not his teacher anymore, so technically we could. It's strange, though...I feel like we're almost past mere dating, as if everything we've been through together up to this point has been taking us inexorably toward a point we haven't yet defined.

Toward an *us*.

I take another swallow of wine, shutting out the voice that wanted to argue that point. Arguing that point with myself eventually cost me my job, right? Regardless of my proud speech to Mr. Kline, I know that he's too young, or at the very least, the circumstances forbid getting involved. My heart and my head are so fucking twisted up on the subject, though.

"We need to hash this out…" I tell my wine glass. "Get straight with one another. Once and for all."

I slouch back into the couch and pick up the remote. Now is a time for Bueller. Bueller, or maybe *The Breakfast Club*. Some eighties angst and humor will remind me of everything good in my life, surely.

Much later, I'm deep in the movie, Gunner still hasn't arrived, and in spite of my brain telling me to relax, I'm worried.

Me: where r u

Re-reading the message I just sent, sober me scoffs at how drunk me doesn't use proper grammar in her text messages. I stare at my phone and then decide to correct it.

Me: Where are YOU You were supposed to be hear an hour ago.no?

Wait. That's not right, either. I give up and push the icon to call him, instead.

Only it rings and rings and apparently, he isn't answering his phone, either, so I can't even call and bless him out. This is very inconsiderate of him, and exactly the reason I do not date.

Tossing my knitting to the side, I stand and start pacing the confines of my living room, wearing a path in the floor as the rainy afternoon shifts into evening. The phone finally buzzes with an incoming text at just after six.

I thumb the screen to read the message, my heart sinking with a sense of foreboding when I see the unknown caller designation that has become so familiar recently. *God. Not again.*

> **Unknown:** A little bird told me you were expecting company.
> **Me:** what did u do
> **Me:** ? you
> **Unknown:** Nothing at all. But I don't think your friend will be making it this evening.

Without replying, I clasp the phone tight in my hands, trying to focus. What do I do? What does he want? The screen goes black, and the wine in my veins starts to chill, sobering me sluggishly.

And then another message illuminates the screen, and I realize it's the blood in my veins turning to ice. Not the wine.

Unknown: Grant Memorial. Room 427. I told you to end it. He won't be as lucky next time.

I sit for a moment in stunned silence. Slowly, my senses start to register input.

The taste of tannin, bitter on my tongue.

The sounds of the Brat Pack, a steady drone in the background.

The colors of the yarn I'd been knitting bright against the dull gray of the sofa.

The smell of the candle I'd lit earlier.

I know that I'll forever associate these things with the feel of my heart breaking. I hadn't realized, until now, that my heart was involved enough to break. I knew there was potential, but until now, I would have sworn I hadn't fallen yet.

I would have been wrong.

I'd fallen, all right. I'd fallen like snowflakes descend from pregnant clouds, slow and steady on their path to the ground. I'd fallen like an evening in the south, a lazy crossing over from dusk to dark. I'd fallen like tears, salt rivers on the bitter topography of a broken heart.

The thought of not seeing him again is a physical ache in my chest. The thought of him being hurt is worse.

Without responding to the text, I go to my bedroom to dress.

Once I'm dressed, I sit on the edge of my bed. My hands are clenched in my lap, trembling despite my grip. I'm not sure I can actually go to the hospital. Aside from being half a bottle of wine too far gone to drive, I don't think I can do this by myself. I haven't been inside a hospital in years, not since Sammy spent so much time in the ICU. The thought of being there again, in that cold, sterile environment, has my stomach in knots.

But who to call?

The thought of Gunner being there, by himself...thinking I don't care...that has me even more twisted up.

I dial Leila.

She arrives in half an hour, during which time I sit and stare at the wall in the living room. When I hear her knock on the door, I rise and gather my coat and purse, opening the door to greet her with mute gratitude.

"Come on, babe. Let's go."

She leads me to her car, and I settle myself in the passenger seat, laying my head back against the seat and closing my eyes as she pulls out of my driveway and onto the road.

"I don't know what to do, Lee."

With my eyes closed, I feel rather than see her eyes touch on me briefly. "Tell me what's going on."

I huff out a breath. "What's not going on? I'm being stalked. For all intents and purposes, I got fired today. I'm falling for a student. And now my stalker is sending messages that basically say ditch that student or see him hurt." Removing my glasses, I rub my temples. "He's hurt now because of me. He's in the hospital because of me."

"Damn, Shy. You go for years being the most boring person I know until all of a sudden—wa-bam. Everything at once."

"I know. It seems like everything just switched on when the school year started."

"Well, that's kind of interesting, isn't it?"

I open my eyes and look at her. "What do you mean?"

"I mean, don't you find it interesting that all of this started after you started teaching? There has to be a connection."

I exhale a shaky breath. "So what do I do?"

"You figure out who's doing this shit to you, that's what you do. Up to this point, everything you've done has been in reaction." She pauses when I look at her in confusion. "He does something, you react. You call the police. You quit your job." I nod and she continues. "It's time for you to *act*, Shiloh. Don't let some creep dictate your relationships or lack thereof. You like this guy?"

"More than like."

"Is he legal?"

A reluctant laugh escapes me. "Yeah. He's legal."

"Then you do you, Shiloh Anne. And after you visit your man, let's visit the club. Take a look at client records."

"I thought Danny already did that?"

Leila huffs. "That man couldn't find his own dick if he tied a string to it. *You* need to look at the records, the names, the copies of their drivers' licenses…see if anything jumps out at you. There may be someone in there going by a different name."

. I nod, worrying my bottom lip between my teeth. "You're right. Let's see how Gunner is doing. Maybe tomorrow will work?"

Leila reaches across the console and grabs my hand, squeezing it tightly. We sit quietly with our respective thoughts until we reach the hospital.

She's right beside me after she parks in the concrete garage, wrapping an arm around my shoulders in a motherly fashion as we walk inside. She chatters non-stop about nothing while we wait on the elevator and then wind our way through the maze of halls to find room 427. It keeps my focus on moving forward, instead of allowing the press of memories to encroach.

And then we're standing at the door of room 427. I hear the low murmur of conversation within, and, raise my hand to knock when the door opens and a nurse strides forward, attention on the tablet in her hands.

"I'll get this information to your doctor, Mr. Ford. You should be good to go within the next fifteen minutes," she says, darting around Leila and me with barely a glance.

Gunner is dressed and sitting on the side of his bed. He looks up as I hover uncertainly in the door, Leila a comforting presence just behind me.

"Shiloh." He makes as if to stand and I go to him quickly, placing my hands lightly on his shoulders to push him back down.

"Don't get up." I feel my lip start to tremble and press my lips together. "God, Gunner, I was so worried. Are you okay?" I answer my own question, tucking my hair behind my ear. "Of course you're not okay…I'm so sorry…"

"Stop it. I'm fine."

"You're not fine! Have you looked at yourself, Gunner?" I soak him in, every bruise, every bandage, his tired eyes.

The skin I can see is mottled with bruises, his forehead raw with an angry red abrasion and a prominent goose egg. White bandage across his nose…is it broken? His cheekbone…I raise a shaking hand to touch his face lightly and he flinches back. "What happened? Did *he* do this?"

"No. I had an accident, right after I got off the phone with you. My windshield was smashed, but mostly intact. I had a few busted lights, some other damage. I couldn't see all that well between the rain and the cracks in the glass and came up on a deer before I saw her. I swerved to avoid her and went down an embankment. I hit a tree and ended up with the worst of the airbag deployment."

To my utter humiliation I can feel tears spill over and snake their way down my face. I grip his arms and slide my hands up, then down, then back up once again and over to his pectoral muscles. Up his neck. He observes me without speaking, eyes steady and watchful. I can't seem to assure myself that he's okay, even with the evidence before me.

"Your nose?"

"Broken, but I'll live. Doc said I'll probably snore." I nod absently, eyes tracing the knot on his forehead, the bruising on his cheekbone. "What about this?"

"Mild concussion. Someone'll have to keep me awake tonight." He tries to leer but there's no concealing the fact that he's in pain.

"I volunteer as tribute," I try to joke, but I can't produce a smile to go with it.

I lift his shirt; there's bound to be more. He flinches slightly but lets me. Bruising stripes his ribs, his chest. I touch it lightly, then more firmly.

The air flees my lungs in a sigh. "You're okay," I mutter, fixing my eyes on the hollow at the base of his throat.

"I'm okay, Shy."

He doesn't understand. "You were in a car accident, though." There's a reason for my restless hands, the desperation behind them.

"But I'm okay. See? Right here. All good." Maybe he does understand, after all.

"You're not dead." With those words, I curl my fingers into the fabric of his shirt and clutch, desperate to hold onto something...anything, and the steady stream of soundless tears turns into a full-on wail. "Oh, my God." I'm almost hyperventilating, the events of the past returning in a swell of feeling that I don't want to deal with.

Lock it up, throw away the key.

I don't want to feel this again.

Gunner carefully pulls my glasses from my face and sets them on the bed before he scoops me up. Dimly I worry that I'm hurting him. I must have said something out loud, because he says "shhh," and pulls my legs around his waist as he walks me to the lone chair in the corner of the room. I sense Leila hovering, and then she's gone, closing the door softly behind her.

I cry. I ugly cry, because redheads are incapable of crying pretty, but Gunner says nothing; just wraps his arms around me and squeezes me tightly to him. He holds me as one would a child, a simple, secure, non-sexual hold that communicates comfort rather than desire. As I sit there, snotting inelegantly all over his tee shirt, I remember doing something very similar several years ago. Once upon a different accident, Gunner sat with me in this same hospital while I wept into his chest, exhausted and scared and worried that my brother wouldn't wake up.

He had to have been worried, too. Even as young as he was, sixteen, I think, he pushed his own fears and uncertainties aside and comforted me, instead. I don't think I ever acknowledged that, or how much better it made me feel.

That was probably the last time I cried.

Finally, there are no more tears. I feel Gunner shifting beneath me, but I am too drained to move. He sits me up a scant inch or two away from him and tugs an honest-to-God handkerchief from his back pocket. He holds it up to my nose. "Blow," he instructs, his voice gruff. With a small, embarrassed laugh, I comply.

He pulls me back so I'm resting against his chest, my ear pressed against the steady thrum of his heartbeat. His hands rub soothing circles on my back.

"I'm sorry," I say, and my voice is thicker than usual. Throaty. "I haven't lost it like that in…well…I guess since the last time I lost it all over you. I think it's just all catching up with me."

"I'm no expert, but it probably needs to, right?" I shrug, and he presses. "I mean, doesn't it feel better just to let it all go?"

I snort. "Jeezus, Gunner. Who's the girl in this relationship, you or me?"

His hands still on my back. "Are we? In a relationship, I mean."

The question brings me full circle to my earlier quest for answers, and I find myself shifting off his lap to stand in front of him. "Wrong thing to ask me right now."

"Why is that?"

"He sent me a text, Gunner."

His hands go to my hips and he dips his forehead to my chest. "Perfect," he mutters. "What did he say?"

In answer I hand him my phone, open to the texts. He lifts his head to read, then tosses the phone behind me to the bed.

"Fuck that, Shy."

I back up, cross my arms over my chest. "We can't just ignore it."

"I'm fine. The only reason I'm here is because I was stupid."

"No, you're fine *this time*. What about the next time? And you didn't do anything stupid—you said you couldn't see out the windshield. He did that, Gunner. Not you."

His fingers clench in the flesh of my hips and he looks up, studying me. "So...what? Is this the excuse you needed? The reason you've been looking for?"

I shake my head. "Of course not. But I can't watch you get hurt because of me, either. I need to do something, Gunner."

The same nurse from earlier pokes her head in. "Excuse the interruption. We were able to speak with your father in California and he spoke with your doctor. Since you're past the age of consent, the doctor released you provided you had a driver." She looks at us in question.

"We're driving him," I answer her.

Gunner rakes a hand through his hair and rises to begin gathering his belongings. "Thank you." The nurse leaves and he returns his attention to me. "We need to do something. You're not alone in this. Did you have something in mind?"

"Leila and I thought we might go to Kendrick's and look through client records. See if anything stands out as unusual, coincidental...that sort of thing."

Gunner nods. "That's a good place to start. Let's do it together, tomorrow." Putting a hand to the small of my back, he begins to steer me out of the room.

"What? No, you have school—"

"I can miss a day. I'd like to help." He looks at Leila. "Is that okay?"

"Of course. We'll just have to get in there when Danny's not there. Sometime before noon?"

"That should work. In the meantime, Shiloh, do you mind if I crash at your place? I will need you to wake me every hour or something." He taps the sheaf of papers the nurse left on the rolling table and against his thigh and rolls them into a tight column.

"Of course, unless you'd rather go home. Did you already call Nonna?" A thought occurs to me. "We should probably message Brodie, too. If he was at my house, he's probably wondering what on earth is going on."

"He messaged me when you guys were walking in; he's good. And yes, Nonna and Esme were here just a while ago. Let's go to your house." He slings an arm carefully across my shoulders. "I need quiet and you. That's all."

I reach up to take hold of his hand, dangling down just over my breast. In reply, I turn it toward my face and press a kiss into his palm.

I'm a fraud, though. On the outside, I'm strong and stable, good with moving forward.

On the inside, I'm a mess and a liar. It's not an excuse. It's a truth, rather, that I can't let Gunner be injured again. If I had to choose between him being physically harmed by my stalker, or having his heart broken by me, I think I'd break his heart in a second if it would keep him safe.

It's no kind of choice, but it may well be the only one I'm given.

4
Shiloh

CUTTING THE ENGINE, I open the car door and climb out. The parking lot at Karli's Kuppa is as dark as it ever is at ten at night, and I hurry toward the building. At least that's brightly lit. I've been craving a Boston crème donut for days now and I've finally given in, even though I had been tucked into bed for an hour already. I pulled a pair of sweats over my sleep shorts and a coat over my camisole and left the house.

It's been nearly a week since Gunner's accident.

We made our visit to Kendrick's to check out the client records but didn't get all the way through the alphabet before the manager, Danny, showed up. We pretended I was there to ask for my job back— which was interesting, because at the time Danny didn't seem too inclined to rehire me. He promised to speak to the owner, though, and he must have followed through, judging from Leila's call last night.

Everything is so awkward, now. There were quite a few familiar names in the files we went through, surprising for the club's distance away from our town. I guess men had no problem traveling over an hour to look at naked women.

Shane Reasor was a client, which was disturbing but not particularly shocking. Then there was Mark Lincoln, a man my mother had dated briefly before she died. And

Trent Samuels, the freaking youth minister at the Presbyterian church.

I had left feeling unsettled and faintly nauseous. I don't like knowing the names and faces of the men I've danced for. The knowledge is an oily residue on my skin, an awareness I can't cleanse myself of. Were they imagining me naked, I wondered, when we ran into each other at Karli's Kuppa or in the produce section of the grocery store?

But no…it wouldn't be imagining, would it? It would be remembering.

My skin crawls, thinking about it.

After going through as many of the club records as we could, and finding nothing helpful, we agreed to a little space until things calmed down.

Or rather, I had stated, and Gunner had glared. But he didn't argue when I said we'd stick to tutoring, and absolutely no more overnights. Brodie would continue to keep an eye on things at night.

So here I am, all by my lonesome in the parking lot at Karli's. Gunner would be pissed, but I texted Brodie to let him know where I was going. I'm sure he's lurking somewhere.

Gunner introduced us officially the night I brough him home from the hospital, and we were able to share a laugh at my behavior weeks past, when I caught him smoking a clove cigarette on the abandoned property across the road from my house. Instead of doing what any reasonable woman being stalked would do—calling the police—I marched myself outside like an idiot, confronting him in a video streaming live on Facebook. That video has since collected a slew of comments regarding my idiocy.

It seemed like a good idea at the time.

My lips quirk, thinking about it.

Now it's that time of the month, and I've learned to cater to my cravings whenever possible. If my body was telling me it wanted a Boston crème donut, there was no doubt some healthy reason for it.

The line is short, thankfully, and it's only a matter of minutes before I'm headed back to my car, half a dozen pastries secure in their box under my arm. Opening the door, I bend and place the box in the passenger seat, then straighten and twist to climb in behind them.

Intent on getting my donuts safely into the car—no Shane Reasor repeats, please—I don't register the form behind me until it slams me into the corner formed by door and car body. I shriek, and a hand immediately clamps over my mouth. A hard male form molds itself to my back, immobilizing me against the car.

"My, my, if it isn't Miss Brookings. Looking fine this evening…" The man's voice is oily with intent and slurred, and I realize he's drunk. I don't recognize his voice, but his identity is the least of my worries as his other hand comes around to pull my coat free and grope with fingers that hurt at my breast. I can't move, pinned as I am. Terror ratchets up as I feel him grind his hardness against my rear, and despite my half-formed resolved to be strong, a whimper escapes into his palm.

He chuckles. "You like it, don't you? Like it rough? I heard all about you…heard you like 'em young. Heard you're a freak between the sheets. Heard—"

Behind his hand, I scream. Damn it, Karli's is *right there*. Am I going to be raped in the parking lot, just yards away? His free hand runs over my body, squeezing and fumbling at my flesh.

Frustrated tears seep from my eyes and I try to open my mouth enough to bite, to no avail. In an effort to dislodge him, I thrash my head from side to side, making myself dizzy and sending sharp pain shooting down my spine. *This can't be happening.*

It's ironic, but the logical part of my brain is saying he's not my stalker. This crude attack doesn't feel right. I'd expect more sophistication, less drunken frat boy.

What are the odds, though, that a woman with a stalker would be attacked by some random in a parking lot? Was God looking for someone to torture? It doesn't make sense...it—

The man is laughing. His hand slips between our bodies and squeezes a cheek roughly. "Oh, yeah, baby. That ass..."

I buck against his hand, but it only serves to excite him further. His hand fumbles at the waistband of my pants, and I brace myself to feel his hand against my skin, screaming again into his palm.

He never touches me. Instead there's the roar of a powerful engine and then another, human roar, before the weight of his body is yanked abruptly off of me. My knees buckle without his weight pressing into me and I sag, turning in time to see Brodie fling him backwards. "OhGodohGodohGod." The words are a prayer as I lean, frozen, half in and half out of the car.

Brodie crashes a fist with efficient brutality once, twice into the man's face, stopping when he sees him go limp. He drops him to the ground, lip curled in disgust, and turns to me.

"Are you okay? I'm so sorry, lass." His brogue is thick.

"Where were you?" A sob escapes and I punch him in the chest. Brodie takes it in stride, pulling me into a cautious hug, one big paw cupping the back of my head.

"I'm so sorry," he repeats. "I had a call from my boss—my other boss, my real one. I can't ignore him."

Pulling away, I walk the few feet to look at my unconscious attacker. He's younger than I imagined, and I realize as I study his slack features that he was a student in one of my classes. He made a suggestive comment to me one day and Gunner shot him down.

"Recognize him? Is he the guy, you think?"

"He was a student of mine," I answer, calmer now that I can identify him. "I don't think it's him, though. His attack was different from the other things the stalker has done. Unplanned, crude...and he's drunk." I can smell the alcohol wafting up from him and turn back to my car. "I think he thought I'd be into it because of Gunner. There was an...incident...at the school not too long ago."

Brodie's expression is troubled as he pulls out his phone. "Let me call Gunner."

"No." It comes out sharper than I intended and with considerable effort, I lower my voice. "I don't care what you do with him," I said pointing to the limp form on the ground, "but Gunner doesn't need to know. It would upset him that, however indirectly, it was his presence in my life that brought this on."

Brodie snaps a photo of the guy. "No promises, lass. I see what you're saying, but he needs to know. And he is my boss."

I slide behind the wheel. "This is just going to create problems."

"Go home, Shiloh. I'll pull him out of the way and be right behind you."

With a nod, I do as he says.

AS I'M STEPPING THROUGH THE DOOR, my phone rings with an incoming Skype call. Cotton's face fills the screen and I answer, dropping my purse and shrugging out of my coat and shoes in the foyer.

"Cotton..." My voice breaks as I say her name and I have to hold the phone away while I compose my expression. I sink down into the couch, pulling the throw blanket over me, and open the box of donuts.

"Shiloh, what the hell? What's going on?"

I take a bite and speak with my mouth full. "What's not going on?" Chew. Swallow. "I'll start at the top—tonight—and work my way backward. After you tell me why you're calling me out of the blue."

"It's not out of the blue, babe. It's Thursday. Geez, you really are out of it, huh?"

"I'm fine. There's just been a lot going on the past several days."

"I'm listening. Talk to me."

"Fine. So, first, I just got assaulted in the parking lot of Karli's."

Cotton gasps. "Are you okay? Why aren't you freaking out? What the hell happened?"

"Believe me, I'm freaking out on the inside. He just came out of nowhere, pinned me to my car and starting t-touching me. Hand was over my mouth, so I couldn't scream. I've never felt so damn helpless in all my life."

"Shiloh—"

"I'm fine. Brodie—a friend—got him off of me. He was a former student—"

"Former?"

"Yes, I lost my job. I'll get there. Just listen, though. He was just a loser who thought since there's a rumor going around that I'm fucking Gunner Ford, I'd be up for anything." Cotton's expression is enraged. I have no doubt that if she were stateside she'd be on her way to whup some ass. "That's why I lost my job, by the way. Because of the rumor. Which is not true, but—"

"Oh, shit."

"Exactly. I can't do this, though, Cotton. It's just not going to work. I like this guy so damn much, but everything is just fucked up. The stalker's bad enough, but now I have—"

"Back up, chickadee. What's going on with this creep? Last I heard, you were short listing Shane Reasor for that role."

"I don't want to talk about it right now. I just want to eat this donut and go to bed. Maybe cry into my pillow."

"You don't cry."

"I do now. I cried at the hospital—"

"You went to the hospital?" She knows how big a deal that is for me. I don't do hospitals. I don't do funerals.

"To see Gunner. The stalker messed with his truck, his beautiful truck, and he had an accident."

Cotton rubs her forehead wearily. "Let me see if I have this all straight. You have feelings for Gunner, and we all know that boy's in love with you. You have a stalker—probably from that stupid Kendrick's—who is… stalking… you, and tampering with motor vehicles. Gunner was injured as a result. And tonight you were attacked by another, somewhat random dude."

I nod and finish off my donut. "That's about right."

"I'm sorry. I'm still stuck on the fact that you were assaulted. Are you sure this guy and the stalker are not one and the same? That's fairly random."

"I thought so, too, and no…of course, I'm not sure. It's just a feeling I have."

"Did you call the police? Go to the hospital?"

"No. He just grabbed me—"

"There's no "just" about any of this, Shy."

"You know what I mean. I may end up with a few bruises, but I'm okay. It just freaked me out. And I didn't call the cops because Brodie was there and knocked him unconscious."

"I think I want to meet this Brodie."

"Yeah, well, y'all would get along. He's probably going to tell Gunner and then Gunner will feel obligated by some male sense of pride to go beat this guy's ass, too…oh, my God. I'm exhausted just thinking about it." I toss my glasses on to the couch and rub my eyes.

Cotton's lips are pressed in a thin line. "Fair enough. But if Gunner doesn't kick his ass, I call dibs."

I groan. "Can we please talk about something else?"

"Fine. Why are you saying this won't work with Gunner? And don't say age. I will reach through this screen and shake you."

"It's more than that. He has his whole life in front of him, and I have…what? A brother I'm responsible for? It's not like I can follow him to college."

"Now, Shiloh, you know that's not going to be forever. And Sammy's improving every day."

I ignore her interjection. "The stalker has threatened him, telling me to distance myself. I've lost my main source of income and am probably skating this close—" I hold up two fingers pinched together. "—to being ostracized by the community. And now I'm getting attacked by random creeps who think I'm open for business." I sink further into the cushions. "There's probably something I'm forgetting."

"No, I think you covered about everything," Cotton responds dryly.

"So, I don't think it's in the cards for us. Not right now." We sit in silence for a few minutes. "I've been tutoring him still, but I should probably just end things with him when I see him tomorrow, huh?"

"Is that what you want to do?" Cotton stops me when I open my mouth to speak. "Be honest with yourself."

I think for a moment. Do I want to end things with him, before they've even truly started? The idea is a physical pain in my chest, like the tightening and heaviness that came with the pneumonia I'd had years ago. I meet Cotton's gaze. "No."

"Then don't, Shiloh. Respect yourself, respect the wishes of your heart. The rest will fall into place."

5

Gunner

SOMETHING'S OFF WITH SHILOH.

We sit across the table from one another, books and school assignments spread out between us, and although she's speaking easily on the academics, she's not meeting my eyes.

I chew thoughtfully on the end of my pencil as she reads through what I've just written, marking suggestions for correction in green ink. She doesn't like red, says that it has negative connotations or something like that.

"You're flipping the dates on these. Instead of 1986 it should be 1968, and so on."

"Got it."

She continues reading, forehead creased in concentration as she checks my paper against the text. She's been here for an hour, and so far, hasn't made one personal statement or observation. Not that I think we need to talk about *us* non-stop or anything, but I can't help thinking it weird for a chick to completely avoid the subject. Even if she kind of lay down the law and say we needed to put a little space between us until this thing with the stalker was resolved.

Not that I ever expressly agreed to that, of course.

And then, of course, there's what happened last night, and the fact that she didn't want me to know. That she has no intention of telling me, according to Brodie.

"I hear Karli's is having a special on donuts this week," I mention.

That scores a response. Her eyes flicker up to meet mine, and in their hazel depths I see fierce emotion simmering. Anger. Fear. With careful movements, she sets her pen down on the table, aligning it precisely with the edge of the textbook, and then folds her arms across her chest.

"Do you have something you wish to discuss, Gunner?"

"Yeah. I do. What made you think you could keep something like that from me? Why didn't you call me last night?"

"It was handled. Brodie was there and he took care of the problem. I didn't see the point in bothering you with it. Especially after I told you I thought we needed to rein things in."

"Bothering me?" I fling the pencil I was toying with down on the table, relishing the small flinch it provokes. "Was it a *bother*, Shiloh, when I was in the hospital getting stitches? Were you thinking, damn that Gunner. Such a *bother*."

"Of course, not. But that was my fault—not yours. And this…" She stops, turning her head and looking out the window.

"This isn't your fault, is it, *dolcezza*? This is my fault."

"No, it's not—"

"I know who exactly who attacked you in that parking lot, Shiloh. And why. It absolutely is my fault for pushing and pushing for you to see me, to feel what I feel, to know what I know."

"That's not—"

"My fault that I wasn't more careful, that punks like him picked up on it."

"It's not your fault! This! This is why I didn't want Brodie to tell you. I didn't want you to blame yourself."

I shrug. "Gotta call it like it is. This is on me. I should have been more discreet." Shiloh doesn't reply. I wish she would yell. Hit me like she did Brodie. The idea of some guy putting his hands on her...I flex my fist, looking at the abraded knuckles. "I took care of the problem."

"What?" She looks at my hand and grabs it, turning it so she can see the knuckles better. "What did you do?"

I meet her gaze, letting her see everything I'm feeling. Remorse. Rage. Resolve. "I made it very clear that you were off limits, that's all."

She drops my hand and stands, gathering her stuff together and shoving it into that bag she carries around with her everywhere. "I can't do this, Gunner." Her voice is choked.

I circle the table, stop her by placing a hand on hers as she packs up. "What can't you do? Where are you going, Shiloh?"

Her eyes, when they meet mine, glisten with moisture. "This." She gestures between us with her free hand. "I can't do you, and me, and us. It's too much. I'm just... I'm so tired, Gunner." She leans her forehead against my chest, and as I wrap my arms around her and pull her into me, I can feel her trembling.

Honestly, I'd been expecting this sooner or later. If Shiloh was ever going to embrace us, I knew she had to work through all the reasons we wouldn't work, first. Confront them, debunk them, and set them aside.

She'd been alone so long; it was only natural that she didn't trust what she was feeling.

Since she'd shown me the text she received at the hospital, I'd had some time to think about it and decide how I was going to allay her fears.

"C'mon." I turn to leave the study, taking her hand to pull her along behind me.

"Where are we going?"

"You'll see."

I stop at the closet in the hall to pull two coats and a couple pairs of gloves out, giving Shiloh a set and keeping one for me. Then I lead her through the kitchen and into the garage. As we pull on coats and gloves, I punch the button to open the bay where my bike is parked and watch Shiloh's eyes widen in surprise.

"You have a motorcycle?"

I grin and hand her a helmet, helping her fit it properly on her head and doing the snaps. "It technically belongs to my dad. He rides very rarely, though." She nods, looking like a bobblehead with the big aqua helmet on her head. "That's Esme's helmet. Have you ever been on a bike?" I ask, settling myself onto the seat with plenty of room for her to climb on behind me.

"No."

She eases herself into position behind me, tentative, as if she's afraid her extra buck twenty will knock the bike over. "Arms around my waist," I instruct. "And scoot forward. I don't bite." Her arms come around me, and I reach behind me to pull her flush against me, smirking beneath my helmet. Heat blooms instantly everywhere we touch, even through our jackets and jeans.

She feels so fucking good pressed up against me like this.

I shift to release the pressure tightening my jeans, and with a roar kick the engine to life. "Hold on," I tell her, and feel the quick clench of her fingers on my abs. Then we're off.

We coast along the curvy mountain road, the chill wind biting against us. I'll never be a die-hard biker, but I love to ride. Love the freedom of it, as cliché as that is. Love the solitude, the way it's just you and your thoughts. Even riding double, there's space to think in the absence of conversation.

I wonder what Shiloh's thinking.

Periodically I take one hand from the handlebars to reach behind me and grip her thigh. She responds with a soft squeeze of her arms around my ribs.

Twenty-ish minutes later, I slow and pull into the county cemetery. Both our mothers are buried here. I've come several times a year since I was little to visit mine, but I'm not sure if Shiloh does the same. The sudden tension in her body tells me she likely does everything she can to avoid it.

Pretending not to notice, I pull to a stop along the road where my mother was laid to rest, and after pulling my helmet off, climb off the bike.

"Why are we here?"

I steady her as she swings her leg over the seat and pulls her own helmet off.

"I like to come here and talk to my mom. Thought we might do it together." I was only four when my mother died from complications with Esme's birth, but I have vague memories of a heart-shaped face and pale gray eyes. Her grave has become something of a sounding board. A place for me to speak out loud all the things I don't say to anyone else.

"I don't do cemeteries, Gunner." She tugs against my hand, trying to pull hers loose from mine, but I pull her forward with me as I walk. Gentle. Inexorable.

When we reach my mother's grave site, I release Shiloh's hand and lower myself to sit. The cold immediately seeps through my jeans, but I ignore it. "Hey, Mama," I begin, hyperaware of the woman behind me. "I thought it was time I came to tell you I met someone. Her name is Shiloh, and I've had a thing for her since I was ten years old, when she climbed out of her mom's car and glared across the yard at me and her little brother."

There's a muffled sound behind me. I can't tell if it's a laugh or a sob, but I keep going. "I think you'd like her. Her mom is up there, too...maybe you guys can meet up and have ambrosia coffee one morning or something. But anyway...I wish you could meet each other. Shiloh's smart and sassy and family means everything to her. Her biggest and most treasured responsibility is taking care of her brother. I'm trying to help, but she's prickly as hell. Full of pride." I pause. "I can hear you thinking. Yes, I'm young. The way I look at it, finding this girl now just means I get to spend more time with her in the long run." Leaning forward, I brush a few leaves clear of the headstone. "She's struggling, though, Mama. Struggling with how intense I am, and how strong this thing between us is. Struggling with what other people might think and say. Struggling with letting go a little and trusting someone other than herself."

There's nothing but silence behind me. By the very vacuum of sound, I can tell she's listening, hardly breathing. "If there's any way you can exert a little influence up there...I'd appreciate it."

I sit for a couple of minutes when I'm finished, just staring at the headstone. Then I stand, brush my pants off, and turn to face Shiloh.

Her face is streaked with tears and I stride swiftly to her, taking her face between my gloved hands and pressing a brief, hard kiss to her lips.

"What am I supposed to say to that?" she complains, hiding her face in my chest. I wrap my arms around her back and rest my chin on the top of her head. "How am I supposed to leave you now?"

"That's simple, *dolcezza*." I use my finger to tilt her face up to mine. "You don't."

6
Gunner

THE NEXT DAY, WE'RE SUPPOSED TO BE STUDYING—or at least, I'm supposed to be studying—but I can't keep my attention from straying to Shiloh. She's sitting across from me, her foot in its boot propped up on a chair, reading a book and twirling a lock of hair around her finger. The lamplight gleams off her chestnut hair, illuminating shadows of deep gold and rich red.

As I allow my eyes to trail without inhibition over her delicately carved features and her lush mouth, she takes her bottom lip between her teeth, gnawing on it in concentration. The sight of her even white teeth sinking into her lip, turning it plump and red, gives me ideas that make my jeans tighten uncomfortably.

A groan escapes me and she looks up, catching my eyes on her. Immediately her spine straightens and her face morphs into prim schoolmarm mode. It doesn't help. In fact, it might even make my situation worse, especially when her hand goes up to straighten her glasses on her freckled nose. "You gotta stop looking like that."

A smirk twists her lips. "You just need to stop looking."

"Not gonna happen. I can't stop." She rolls her eyes. "Let's go out. Dinner. A movie. Roller skating."

She snorts at the last suggestion but bites her lip again and looks back down at her book, and I can feel her refusal forming before she says the words. "Not a good idea, Gunner."

Fuck. I thought we'd made headway yesterday at the cemetery. Thought—hoped—that maybe this foolishness with needing space was dead.

"Why not? You're not my teacher anymore, Shiloh," I remind her gently. She tenses.

"I know that. It's more than just that. It's not a good idea to flaunt anything right now. Not after that text." She pauses, draws in a deep breath, then continues. "In fact, I've been revisiting the idea that we need a little distance. I don't want us to get attached, Gunner. It won't end well."

Too late, I think. I sit back in my seat, abandoning all pretense of schoolwork. "You know, I knew when we left yesterday that you weren't all the way there with me, but I wasn't expecting a complete one-eighty."

Unease is plain on her face. "I don't want to do this right now."

I smile. "We need to if we're going to see that movie later, *dolcezza*. Now, come on. What's the problem? Is it just the stalker thing? Or is it more? Is it our ages?"

She puts her elbows on the table and lowers her face into her hands, tugging at her hand. "Jesus, you're persistent." When I remain silent, cocking an eyebrow in reaction, she continues, using her hands like a balance scale to illustrate her point. "The stalker's a big part of it. Age is less important but does weigh on me. It's more, though. It's about where you are and where I am. Maybe where we're headed. You'll be heading off to college soon. You have no idea what that's like—all the opportunities that open up to you. And just three days ago, I *was* your teacher. People would have a field day with that fact if we started dating."

Her gaze, when she looks at me, is apologetic, as if she's sorry she has all these reasons. I stand. "Anything else?"

She replies, her voice barely a whisper and her eyes fixed unblinking on the table in front of her. "Yes. I don't deserve you, Gunner. Up until a few days ago I was a stripper, and that information is out there now. People know. I would die if that choice ever reflected on you…damaged your credibility or your family's business. If people mocked you for having a stripper girlfriend. If your father knew…"

I look past Shiloh, out the window, as I consider her objections. I think I can work around everything except her own sense of shame. With that, all I can do is prove how little it matters to me that she once took her clothes off for cash. That was then. This is now.

Holding up a finger, I say, "Hold that thought."

Several minutes later, I return, Esme in tow. "Esme's going to keep you company for a while." Esme's eyes gleam with mischief and I tug her ponytail. "Be good, Es."

"I'm always good," she replies.

"I see confidence runs in the family," Shiloh responds. Esme waggles her brows and plops herself down next to Shiloh, immediately starting to run her mouth. My sister is a precocious brat, and completely amazing. She'll keep Shiloh occupied for me for a while as I put a few things in motion.

The Win Shiloh Campaign I started years ago isn't over yet.

Shiloh

"YOU LIKE ZOMBIES?"

Unnerved by Esme's lightning fast tendency to bounce from subject to subject, I nod slowly. "Yes. As long as they're not eating my flesh, sure."

"Let's go watch *The Walking Dead*, then. Gunner will be a little while."

"You don't have to babysit me, Esme. I have a book I can read while I wait."

"Oh, I'm not. Besides, I need to get to know you. After all, if we can't stand each other, you and Gunner can't get married."

She startles a laugh out of me. "We are nowhere near that stage, I promise you."

"Uh, huh. Gunner and Shiloh, sitting in a tree. K-I-S-S-I-N-G."

"You're killing me, kid." I trail after her as she leads the way to a cozy room with comfortable furniture and a huge television. She throws herself into one corner of the couch and I follow suit.

"First comes love..." She flicks the television on and we immerse ourselves in zombies and survival. Midway through the episode, she speaks. "So, what's your plan for the zombie apocalypse?"

Again, she makes me laugh, but I consider the question as seriously as possible, tapping my bottom lip with my finger. "I believe the most intelligent course of action in a zombie apocalypse is to find an island, preferably one with a couple of well-stocked, luxurious homes, a garden, and some chickens. It'd be great if it had a forge, too. And then stay put." Her fist shoots out and I tap it hesitantly.

"You pass. If the world started going to shit, I would go immediately to the hardware store and buy a generator and some vegetable seeds. Then I'd pack up an RV and head for the coast."

"Not sure about the RV—those don't have optimal maneuverability. But whatever we're driving, we'd need to store up and carry some gasoline, too. You know the gas stations are going to be overrun."

"And there won't be any power. It'll be a madhouse."

We're quiet for a moment, thinking. Then both of us speak at the same time.

"Back roads!"

"No interstates!"

Esme falls back into the couch cushions, giggling uncontrollably, and I'm reminded of how young she is. "We're definitely going to weather the apocalypse together, Shiloh." We fall into companionable silence as we watch the show, except for the infrequent comment.

"So, any idea what your brother is up to?" We've watched a couple of episodes and I'm starting to wonder.

Esme shrugs. "No idea, honestly. He said he had a couple of errands to run and told me to bring you over to the winery around seven." She glances down at her phone. "Which is very near. Let's go."

Several minutes later we are settled in a golf cart, a cold wind blowing across as Esme steers with confidence over several pebbled paths to get us to the winery. She talks non-stop on the short drive over to the winery, filling my ears with chatter.

"So. You and my brother. Is it serious?" She pins me with intense blue-gray eyes, so like her brothers. The right front tire of the golf cart catches the edge of the path when she looks at me a second too long and I grab the oh shit handle, laughing nervously.

"Ah…it's complicated?" I try.

"Nope. Not good enough." Her head whips back and forth. "You realize that he is completely nuts for you, right?"

"Everything he says and does shows me how much he cares, yes."

"But?"

I sigh. "It's just a lot, Esme. I don't really know how to explain it, and I don't expect you to understand, especially not after a five-minute conversation. I've got a lot of stuff to work through. And I don't know what he wants, to be honest."

Esme looks mischievous. "Besides your babies, you mean?" I whip my neck around to look at her in alarm. "Kidding, kidding! Lighten up! Shiloh… just…you need to relax. I know you have responsibilities. He's not asking you to run away to his castle in the sky and live happily ever after. Just…live a little, right here. Right now." She stops in front of the winery and hops out while I sit, stunned by the wisdom that just came from her young mouth.

"Did Gunner put you up to this?"

"Nope," she says, popping the p. "I'm just gifted." Rolling my eyes, I climb out and pause for a moment just to take it in.

The winery is a charming stone and white stucco building with a copper roof, encircled with wide paved paths where customers can walk and gather together. Ivy climbs a trellis near the double wooden doors and frames a wide window with diagonal iron mullions, an unexpected, old world touch of nostalgia that captivates me.

Esme's already disappearing inside. I follow and hear her belting out Gunner's name as she enters a reception area. There's a large wooden bar against one wall, wooden stools lining them like eager patrons. A massive stone fireplace, big enough for me to walk inside, dominates the far wall, a grouping of chairs and couches around it inviting visitors to take a seat. The rest of the spacious room is filled with cozy groupings of leather chairs and intimate tables and seating arrangements. I can imagine that during the busy season this space is filled with people laughing and talking and having a good time with each other.

Gunner enters from a doorway I hadn't yet noticed in the corner. "Hey. Thanks, kiddo." He tugs Esme's ponytail. "You can leave now."

"Wow. Okay. I see I'm loved." Waving good-naturedly, Esme leaves.

And then it's just me and Gunner, the weight of unasked questions between us. I brace myself, and then turn to face him.

7
Shiloh

"So, what is this all about?"

Taking my face in his hands, he pins me with his gaze. He boosts me up on the counter, leaning in between my thighs and wrapping his arms around my waist. "I figured if you weren't comfortable going out in public, I'd bring the date to you."

"Oh."

"Just 'oh'?" he teases.

"No! I'm...this is really sweet, Gunner."

"I just want you to know that I'm listening to you. I don't take anything you've been saying, anything you've been worrying over lightly. I figured we could talk about all of those things, and hopefully set your mind at ease." He pauses, looks up at the ceiling playfully. "And we could eat. And maybe make out."

I start to speak, to tell him that talking isn't going to work out everything that's stacked against us, but with a finger to my jaw he turns my head so I have a sight line into the next room. It's dim, with heavy wood accents and a colorful rug beneath several small round tables. It looks like a private gathering room. I see a table set for two, complete with a glowing candle in its center. There's a familiar red and white bucket in between two plates and now that I'm aware of it, I can also smell the colonel's recipe.

"Oh." His words and actions floor me, send me spinning. He's hammering at those walls, widening the chinks in my defenses. He's refusing to let me run, refusing to let me hide. I take a deep breath. "Okay, then. You had me at fried chicken."

Grinning, he sets me on the floor and we move to the table. We seat ourselves, Gunner pulling my chair out and helping me push it up to the table. His manners, courtly and old-fashioned, never fail to stir warmth in my chest. He always opens the door to his truck for me, waits until I'm seated, and pulls the seatbelt snug across my lap. At first it was annoying. Did he think I couldn't buckle my own seatbelt? What am I, three? But it wasn't long before I started to see it for what it was—a way for him to take care of me.

Gunner's a protector. A caretaker. Two qualities I never saw in my own father and am amazed to see in a high school senior.

As he begins to talk, he opens the bucket and serves us. "So, the first thing I think we need to discuss, and then never talk about again, is this age thing." I nod. "It's three years, Shy. I'm almost nineteen; you're twenty-two, right? This is a ridiculous thing to be concerned about. Would you bat an eyelash if it were reversed, if I were three years older than you?"

"No." I hate admitting to myself that I'm being sexist, but he's right. "It's more that you're young, period, though. I don't understand..." I stop in frustration, not knowing exactly how to phrase the thing that nags at me. "Why? "What is it about an older woman that you like? You should be out there going to parties with your friends, but the closest to that I've ever seen is you at Kendricks. You never talk about going off to college, I never see you just hanging out and acting...dumb."

He rolls his eyes. "One, it's not that I want to be with a quote-unquote *older* woman. You're not old enough to earn the cougar qualification, Shiloh. Sorry. But if you want to know why I'm interested in being with *you*, then it's because you're sweet and beautiful and…all those things I said at the cemetery. And you're complicated. It keeps me on my toes."

I narrow my eyes at him and bite into my chicken. "Complicated. That sounds like a bad thing."

"No! You're like an onion with all these layers and—"

I can't help it; I laugh. "It just keeps getting better."

"A very sexy onion. And every time I peel back one layer and find another, it's like winning the fucking lottery." I put my drumstick on my plate and wipe my fingers, nervous, suddenly, at the intensity with which Gunner is focused on me. He looks at me like there's nothing that could possibly divert his attention, like I'm the only woman in the world. "Do you remember what I told you when your car had been messed with and I took you home?"

I tilt my head, thinking. Most of what I remember from that day is Gunner leaning into me as we stood in my doorway, tormenting me with his promises and his heat.

"I told you how much I loved your uptight schoolmarm side," he continues when I shake my head. "The nerdy girl who doesn't understand her own appeal. But then there's this other Shiloh, hidden just beneath, that's pure seduction."

I feel my face heating. Why is being described as an onion getting to me?

Gunner is still talking. "And then there's my favorite layer of them all, the one that got me when I was ten years-old. The one underneath all of the others, that's tender and vulnerable and trying so hard to protect herself. At heart, Shiloh, you're still my best friend's sister, hurting and trying not to show it."

He falls silent, and I release a shaky breath. How does he do that? See me so plainly when no one else does? It's unnerving. If I'm not careful—

I shake my head, dismissing the thought, and take a big bite of my drumstick. "This is great chicken."

Gunner huffs out a laugh and picks up his own chicken. "And she's back."

Shame assails me. He's laying himself bare and I can't even give him the dignity of letting him see how it affects me. "It's not easy to look at myself the way you see me, Gunner. It's like you have me on this pedestal and—"

"Oh, don't get me wrong. You're stubborn and frustrating as hell most of the time. But you're you. You're the one that I want. You're the one I've always wanted. Good enough?"

"Good enough," I whisper.

"Okay, so you've also always objected to the fact that I'm your student and you're my teacher."

"I'm starting to feel like this is a well-crafted sneak attack..." I smile to soften the snark.

He leans in close and brushes his lips in the barest of caresses against mine. It's a tease and I hate it and love it at the same time. "Yes, well...as I've said before, you're not my teacher anymore, Shiloh." I swallow as he draws back. "You need to stop worrying about what people are going to think. Other peoples' opinions, feelings…they have no place in my relationship with you. I'm not looking for anyone's consent and I could care less about anyone's disapproval." He raises his eyebrow and I chew thoughtfully. Technically, he's correct. I don't have anyone I particularly need to please, except Sammy and Cotton. And something tells me they would love it far too much if we were together.

I give him a short nod. "Fair enough."

"Next. You're afraid. Afraid that this is some kind of game. Afraid that it's not real." His hand creeps across the table and he takes my hand in his. "This is real, Shiloh. All I can do is keep on telling you, *dolcezza*, keep on proving it to you, every day. My family knows how crazy I am for you. My friends see it. The only one blind to it is you." I look down, and he tilts my chin back up with a single finger. "Look at me." When I comply, he continues. "I'm not those assholes your mom investigated when you were waiting in the car—the cheating, abusive spouses and the deadbeats who refused to pay their child support. I'm not your dad. I'm not Shane Reasor. I'm yours, and you can trust me. Got it?" Chewing my lip, I nod.

"Next. The future. Now let me make sure I have this one straight. You're worried because of your job, Sammy, where you see me going, right?"

"Kind of. The biggest thing is my responsibility to Sammy. That's not going away, and it's not fair to push that off on anyone else. It's a legal, financial, and time responsibility."

"All right. You have to know I would never begrudge that, Shy. Sammy's my friend. You can't possibly think I'm such an asshole that I wouldn't be willing to share that with you."

"But, Gunner, you have no concept of how expensive his care—"

"I don't care, Shiloh. Stop talking to me about money. This isn't about money. It's about people."

"Fine. Basically, what you're saying is that you have no problem being a parent right now, you get that, right?" The words feel strangely intimate, but I want to make sure Gunner understands the level of commitment he's avowing to. He doesn't blink.

"Yes."

"Because he's not in a position to pal around with. He has to be cared for."

"I said yes." I wait, and finally accept the truth of his words, the tension in my shoulders deflating as I give in.

"Okay, fine. You're weird; I give up. But what about college? You'll be leaving soon. You'll go away, and find some cute coed, and I'll be last night's leftovers."

"Is that right?" Gunner's crooked smile spreads slow across his face, denting the dimple in his chin.

"Yeah."

"That's not me, Shiloh. I'm not like Miles and other high school guys, thinking about the next chick, the next game, the next party. I don't think I've ever come right out and told you before, but I've been working here at the vineyard for a while now. I've always known where I'm going, what I'm doing. It's always clicked for me. This — our vineyard — is it. It's my future." His voice lowers, deepens, and that rasp that sets my nerve endings on fire does it again, raising gooseflesh along my arms. "The first time I saw you, Shiloh, you clicked right into place with everything else, and I just knew."

"But—" My objection stops as Gunner rises abruptly and comes to kneel in front of me.

"I looked at you across your mom's yard, and I told Sammy, *I'm going to marry your sister one day*."

I have to laugh. "You did not."

"Okay, you got me. I told him that after we played seven minutes in heaven. He gave us his blessing, if you're curious."

"Gunner—"

"And I don't give a shit that you were a stripper, Shiloh. My dad wouldn't give a shit if he knew. The only feelings that matter are mine for you and yours for me." It's as if he knew what I was going to say. He stares intently into my eyes, willing me to understand, to give in. "Do you feel it, Shiloh, this same thing I'm feeling?"

"Gunner." I whisper, setting my hand over his heart. It beats a rapid tattoo under my palm, and I know if I were to touch two fingers to my pulse, I'd feel the same fast rhythm.

"Shiloh," he returns.

"I feel it, too, Gunner. But I can't see this being easy."

He laughs a little. "Shiloh, I don't want easy. I want hard. And crazy. And every beautiful thing that's you. Can we do that? Can we try?"

Looking up at him, his lips so close and his fingers gripping my hips hard with desperation, I nod. "I'll try." Then I close my eyes and sink into him. *We're doing this*, I think, my heart beating fast and hard. *I'm officially stupid for this boy.*

I'M NOT YOUR DAD. I'M NOT SHANE REASOR.

Gunner has no idea what those words do to me. Or maybe he does, I don't know.

Dad did a number on my ability to trust, first with his own unfaithfulness to my mother, and then when he took me away from her and Sammy for close to a decade. He wanted to work in the California branch of his company and when mom wouldn't go after him, he did the only thing he thought would work in retaliation—gaining custody of me.

It was an asshole move, especially since he didn't have the first clue about how to raise a pre-pubescent girl. It was almost a relief when he died and I returned to Virginia.

Shane Reasor hadn't helped matters when he took Krystal Jenkins into the school supply closet barely a month after we'd started going out. I still find that one hard to believe. He had fought so hard to get me to go out with him in the first place, bringing me donuts from Karli's every day until I caved, only to screw it up royally by being unfaithful when I wasn't ready to have sex immediately.

I shrug my coat off as I step into the house, locking my door with its shiny new deadbolt behind me.

I have to give Gunner points; he's persistent and painfully honest—about his feelings, at least. There was that whole thing with telling me his sister had dyslexia, instead of him. I was irritated at the time, but looking back, I understood. Women were all about feelings, but I was learning that guys were all wrapped up in their pride. Their ego. A blow to the pride was, to a man, comparable to a woman getting her heart broken. It had taken Gunner a while before he was able to believe it would be all right to humble that pride to me. He did, though.

The ancient grandfather clock in the living room chimes the hour as I pull a wine glass from the cabinet and open the fridge for the wine. Ten o'clock. Just enough time to relax before I head to bed.

I love these quiet evenings, when most of the house is draped in shadows and there's no one around to make me talk. All I have to do is whatever I want.

And right now, that's have a glass of wine and go to bed.

I'm half-asleep, lulled by the stillness of the night, when my phone rings. Glancing at the display, I slide to answer.

"Hey, Leila. Everything okay?"

"Of course, baby, why—oh, crap. I didn't look at the time. I'm sorry. I'll be quick. Have you found another job yet?" Words tumble one over the next, classic Leila style.

"No, not really. I've been playing with the idea of picking up my photography again—"

"Good! We lost a girl tonight. Can you come back?"

"Ah…yes? Sure. Who did we lose, and how? And why isn't Danny calling me?"

She sniffs. "He was a dick to you the other day. I told him I'd call you. And we lost Monica. She took some temp job in Richmond."

"Oh. Okay, then. When do you need me?"

"Tomorrow?"

After I get a few further details, we disconnect. I sit, holding the phone loosely in my lap. I'll have to let Gunner know and I don't want to. He's not going to be happy, but he'll have to get over it. My bills won't wait.

After a moment of thought, I tap out a text. I'll give him a heads up, at least.

Me: Hey. You there?
Gunner: for u always
Me: I wanted to let you know; Danny offered my job back. I start tomorrow night.

Three dots appear and dance before disappearing, and then the phone rings.

"Hello?"

"You're not going back to that place."

Temper spikes immediately and I rise to pace the small living room. "You don't get to make that decision for me, Gunner."

"Over my cold dead fucking body will you be taking your clothes off for any other man, Shiloh Anne Brookings."

"Stop acting like a caveman." I can picture him in his house, tugging at his hair the way he did when he was frustrated. "I quit for you before and lost my job anyway. I don't have a lot of options at the moment."

"Hell, Shiloh. You have plenty of options. Do some photography—"

"One does not just 'do some photography,' Gunner. Don't you think I may have tried that in the beginning? That was my dream. It takes time to make a name for yourself, and until you do, you end up doing a lot of free work."

He grunts. "What about teaching dance at the studio downtown?"

"I called the day after I left the high school. Miss Lily is going to let me teach a class twice a week, but she doesn't have enough students to bring me in full-time. We're working on the details, getting sign-ups and stuff now. It will help. But it's not enough."

"More tutoring?"

"I wouldn't mind that," I admitted. "But again, it'll take a little time to build a clientele. Time I don't have." I pause, draw in a deep breath. "I have to do this, Gunner. At least for right now."

"*Dolcezza.*" The anger is gone from Gunner's voice. He just sounds tired. Done. "Don't do this to me. I can't…"

"It's not for forever. I promise."

Click. He disconnects, and I'm left listening to dead air. As I turn my own phone off and plug it in to charge for the night, I can't help but wonder if it's an omen. Pushing the thought away, I dump my wine down the sink, turn off the lights, and go to bed, feeling horrible.

8
Gunner

AFTER I DISCONNECT WITH SHILOH, I CALL MILES. I'm about to lose my shit. I need his help to ensure Shiloh doesn't get up on that stage tomorrow or any other night. I'm pretty sure that if she does, I'll go Neanderthal and haul her off.

Miles answers. "Hey, man. What's up?"

I run my fingers through my hair. "Hey. I need a favor."

"What's up?"

I give him a quick run-down of my conversation with Shiloh. "So long story short, I need to make sure she doesn't do it. I'm not going to handle it very well if she does, you know?"

"I don't blame you. I wouldn't be okay with any of it, either. If Sherry suddenly took it into her head to take her clothes off for other guys, I'd shit a brick." He falls silent.

"The crazy thing is that it's not even the fact that she's taking them off, you know. As much as I hate it, that's her choice. It's more that other guys are looking at what's mine. I don't care if they've seen before a hundred times. Licked it, kissed it, screwed it...she's *mine* now. I need to be the only one looking."

And that was it, the thing that Shiloh didn't understand, and I was shit at explaining. I wasn't trying to deny her the ability to do whatever she wanted with her body. I was trying to keep myself from ending up in jail if I caught another man looking at her, fantasizing about her.

"I get it. So, what do you want to do? Want me to tell Dad not to hire her back?"

I think for a minute. "No…she needs the money. Is there somewhere he can put her so she's not stripping?"

"How about I tell him she needs to be behind the bar? She can apprentice under Teddy until she picks it up, then work her own shifts, maybe lunch hour."

Relief washes over me. "Yes. That sounds perfect. She's going to kill me, but thanks, brother."

Shiloh

THE CLUB IS DIM AND QUIET WHEN I ENTER THIS AFTERNOON. I walk through, murmuring a low greeting to Teddy, the bartender, who's occupied with restocking his liquor supply. Trailing my fingers along the chair backs as I head toward the back, I breathe in the scent of the club. It has its own unique smell, a lingering, not-unpleasant scent of man blended with cigar smoke. I love the club when it's like this, silent and near empty of humanity, the lights dim and the stage bare. It seems shrouded in mystery and even romance, full of anticipation for the evening ahead but none of the base reality.

It makes me want to photograph it, capture this essence before it shifts and changes. It would make for an interesting study to compare a photo story of the two disparate club personalities. I make a note to bring my camera with me next shift and indulge myself.

For the first time since I lost my teaching job, I feel a tiny spark of hope. Maybe I can do something with my photography. It wouldn't take off immediately, of course, but I could bridge that gap with the tutoring and the job here at Kendrick's. But there were piles of photographers out there on Instagram, making a living as influencers with advertising. I just needed something to set me apart.

Walking past the stage, I enter the hallway and walk into Danny's office. He's sitting at his desk, sorting through a stack of receipts and grumbling to himself.

"Hey, Danny." I plop myself down in the chair across from the desk and wait.

"Shiloh! Welcome back. Looking good, sweetheart."

"Thanks, Danny. And thanks for giving me my job back."

"Other plans didn't work out?"

I avoid his gaze, ignore the slightly snide tone in his voice. He doesn't need to know about my teaching job or my relationship woes. "No. Not really." Shrugging, I change the subject. "Do you have my line-up for tonight? I'll get my costumes pulled together and do some warm-ups."

For the first time since I sat down in his office, Danny looks uncomfortable. "Actually, Shiloh, there's been a change in scheduling. I put you on the bar tonight, helping Teddy."

"The bar?" I'm confused. "When I first applied and wanted to bar tend, you said that Kendrick's didn't put multiple tenders at the bar and it was covered."

"Yeah, well, we've had some changes issued by the boss. So, bartending it is. You should be happy, yeah? This is what you came here for years ago, not stripping."

"Well, yeah. I guess I'm just surprised. It seems strange."

"Just be happy with it. I got the impression Mr. Kendrick really didn't want to hire you back, to be honest."

"Huh. Okay, then." I raise my hands in a placating manner. "I'm happy."

"Head on out whenever you're ready and Teddy'll start teaching you the ropes. Black pants, white tuxedo halter for uniform. It should be at your station already."

"Okay. Thanks, Danny."

TENDING BAR IS INSANE. Likely not as crazy as it might be in some happening club spot, but busy enough to make my head spin. There's a steady stream of customers, mostly men, but plenty accompanied by women. They order drinks with bizarre names, ask endlessly for refills, and wave cash to get our attention. And then there are the cocktail waitresses, arriving non-stop with table orders to be filled.

Teddy puts me on cocktail waitress duty, and I spend most of the evening filling their rapid-fire orders. I have to Google how to mix most of the drinks, which slows me down, but everyone is mostly patient, and I find I'm enjoying the rush. It's nice, too, to see my old colleagues.

"So, you really do tend bar here." I look up from the drink I'm building at the sardonic statement and see Shane Reasor slouched over the polished wood surface of the bar. I tip my chin at him.

"Shane. How nice to see you." Sarcasm is thick in my words. He's already sipping a beer, so I don't ask if he needs anything.

"I'm sorry, Shiloh."

I look up at him coolly. "For what, Shane? You were just doing your job, right?"

He twists his drink in his hands, running a finger through the condensation. "That's just it. I knew you worked here—"

"That's awkward."

He smirks. "For you maybe. Not for me. But anyway. I didn't...I would never have said anything to anyone about it." Heat stains his cheeks, and I turn and hand the tray off to the waitress, starting another order immediately. "I'm not a snitch."

"Then what was all that business in the office? Why were you even in there?"

He shrugs helplessly. "I don't even know. I think he wanted a witness and I happened to be in the wrong place at the wrong time. I tried to tell him I didn't think it was appropriate and he told me to sit down."

Oddly, I believe him. Although even if he's not a snitch, he's absolutely a perv.

"Okay," I say. "Question is, then—who did? Any ideas on who might have done all that to my classroom? Are they investigating?"

Shane scratches his head. "I wish I did. That was some kind of messed up. And there was an attempt at investigation. It didn't go very far."

"What about camera footage?"

"Apparently there was none. Glitch in the system that night."

"Of course, there was." My lips thin.

Shane lapses into silence as I work, thinking. "It's gotta be someone you know, right?"

My immediate reaction is *hell, no*. There's no way someone I know would do this stuff to me. It's sick. Twisted. I don't know people like that. I shake my head decisively. "No. I don't know anyone that's messed up like that, Shane. I mean, I would sense that, I would think. And it could just be someone here, like a client—"

It's Shane's turn to shake his head. "I don't think so, Shiloh. That shit in your classroom was personal. Angry. And this is the kind of shit that gets people locked up. He'd have to be pretty skilled at hiding it in order to be a functioning member of society. People don't wear their crazy on the outside."

A chill skitters down my spine. "Mm. Maybe. Thanks for making me feel super safe right now, Shane."

Shane takes a long draw on his beer. "Sorry." He turns around and props his elbows on the bar, surveying the crowd. "Just trying to help you open your eyes and see what's around you."

Drinks finished, I set them on the waitress's tray and study the crowd with him. I've gone largely unnoticed tonight, being dressed and behind the bar. I scan for familiar faces, or anyone that appears to be looking at me too intently.

The only one I see is Gunner. He sits by himself at a table against a wall, sipping on a drink as he has been since he drove me here for my shift. He refused to let me go alone, and part of me was glad, even though I gave him plenty of grief over his high-handedness. His eyes aren't on me at the moment, but I've felt his gaze all night. I haven't seen him look at a dancer a single time.

Even after Shane wanders away and I return to making drinks, I watch. And wonder, uneasily, if my stalker hasn't been right under my nose the entire time.

9
Him

TONIGHT'S THE NIGHT I SAY GOOD-BYE TO SWEET LITTLE MADISON. I'm almost sorry to see her go.

Almost.

She's been a docile pet, has done everything absolutely perfectly. Maybe that's the problem. I'm bored.

Maybe it's that I feel like I'm being unfaithful, knowing as I do she's only a substitute for the one I really want.

Maybe it's that Shiloh is back where she's supposed to be, and yet...not. She's not where I want her, but is hiding, instead, behind the bar. She's not supposed to be doing something so mundane. She should be on the stage, or in a peep box, dancing. For me.

That she's not sends rage spiking through me, but I tamp it down. It's all right. I'll have her soon enough and she'll dance for me until her feet bleed. All of the pieces are falling nicely into place...just a small nudge here and there is needed to direct them.

I'll start with getting rid of Madison so I can stop fucking around and concentrate on Shiloh.

It's time.

After entering the cabin, I flick on the lamps in the common area and then set about setting the scene. Tonight is important, and appearances must reflect that.

I lay a crisp white cloth across the plain wood of the dining table and set two tapers an equal distance apart. Each place is set with fine bone china and authentic silver. After transferring it to a serving dish, I place the meal in the center of the place settings, and then stand back to take stock.

Perfect.

I pull the cuffs on my button up shirt and straighten my already straight collar. It's time.

"Madison…" I croon, opening the door of the cellar and shining my phone's flashlight into the darkness. I know she's heard me up here moving about, but she's been quiet. She knows not to make any noise. "Did you miss me, sweetheart?"

She whimpers and there's a rustle of sound, as though she's moving. A moment later, her eyes shine in the glare of the light and she throws a hand up to shield them. "Y-y-yes," she whispers, her voice rough with disuse, and I frown. She sounds weak.

I release the mechanism holding the ladder-steps and they lever themselves to the floor. "Come." Standing, I train the light on the steps and wait for her to reach the top.

It takes her forever, and when she finally pulls herself to the edge, her arms are quivering with effort. She's still naked from my last visit, and in the lamp light I can see the blue tinge to her lips.

Must be cold down there.

She's moving too slowly. Impatient with the delay, I take hold of her arm and pull her the rest of the way up, kicking the trap door closed once she's sprawled on the floor at my feet.

"Come, Madison. Let's sit at the table." I move in that direction and tug a chair out, motioning for her to sit. Never let it be said that Mother didn't raise me to be a gentleman. "I'm sure you're famished. I've put together a nice meal for us." I seat myself opposite her, the candle in the center of the table gleaming off of the place settings and glassware. Madison's eyes are dull and wary as they track from one item to the next.

"I don't think I'm very hungry," she admits, crossing her arms over her chest.

I tsk. "Your ribs are showing. Of course, you're hungry."

I spoon sauce over the veal I picked up from our sole Italian restaurant and plate it, along with a helping of pasta. I pour us each a generous splash of wine and reach across the table to lift her napkin and shake it free of its folds. "Eat."

She takes the napkin and places it obediently in her lap, then picks up her fork. I watch as she spears a tiny bite of meat and brings it to her lips. Irritation rises within me.

"It's a shame," I begin, wrapping a skein of spaghetti around the tines of my fork. "...that you weren't...*more*, Madison. Do you understand what I mean?" She shakes her head, mute, and I scoff. "Take that, for example. When I ask a simple question, you quiver like a startled rabbit, and shake your head. Where are your words, Madison? Where is your spirit?"

If possible, she shrinks even further into herself, setting the fork down and curling her shoulders inward. "I'm sorry," she whispers. "I'm trying, but I don't—"

"I'm sorry," I cut her off, my words a mockery of hers. "I'm trying..." My mouth twists in a sneer and I take a sip of my wine. "I would have placed you on a pedestal, Madison. Cherished you with more than just darkness. I wanted to make you a queen."

Madison looks at me in confusion and I stare into the lamplit room beyond the naked girl trembling before me, a vision rising in my mind's eye. Sensuous curves. Soft, pale skin. Hair like a burnished penny. So real, she could almost be standing before me.

Abruptly I yank my eyes back to Madison. "Someone else showed me what a queen truly is, though. You...you're nothing but a shadow."

"I-I'm sorry," she stammers again. "I'll do better, I promise."

I stand, and she stutters to a stop. "No," I tell her. "Your time is up. Madison, you have been tried, and you have been found wanting."

"What are you—"

"Tonight, you will be sentenced." Dramatic? Perhaps. I'm heady on the authority in my own voice, though. In the fear it evokes in the girl before me.

"—doing? I've been a good girl! I've done everything you asked of me—" She stops, choking back a sob. "Please."

"Enough of that. Queens don't beg."

After a moment she takes the hand I extend and allows me to lead her to the bedroom. Her eyes go immediately to the bed and I almost laugh. I have no interest in her that way.

Not since Shiloh, anyway.

I direct her to the bathroom, where I've laid a neatly folded towel, a bar of soap, and a white cotton gown on top of the sink. "Take a shower," I tell her. "Get yourself clean, and then dress in the gown I've left for you."

She blinks rapidly and looks around, wondering, maybe what the catch is. Then a flare of something like hope lights her eyes as she looks at the items on the counter. "Will you...are you letting me go, then?"

I pass a hand down her tangled hair until I'm toying with the ends. "Yes, Madison. I'm going to release you." The words are gentle, and if she chooses to ignore the pity layered beneath the literal meaning, well...that's why she's unworthy. "Be sure to comb your hair. Can't have you looking unkempt."

Turning, I retrace my steps to the bedroom and lie down upon the bed. There's no need for me to watch her this time. Nails, along with a thin stripe of paint, hold the window closed, and I've left nothing she can use as a weapon. I even removed the tank lid, placing it under the bed.

The shower turns on, and from the open door I hear the spray of water against the shower curtain. I've given her that luxury tonight. While she's showering, I blank my mind, eyes fixed on the stippled ceiling above me. The ceiling fan I installed for close summer nights moves in languid circles, barely moving the air.

It's so quiet here that even its gentle electric hum is loud against the backdrop of water on plastic.

Ten minutes later, Madison stands in the doorway, dampness spotting the long-sleeved shift dress I gave her to wear. It's obvious that she didn't take the time to dry herself properly. She's combed her hair, though. It hangs in wet blonde ropes around her too-thin face.

"Good girl," I murmur, swinging my legs off the bed and rising. "Let's go."

Her eagerness, as she follows me like a dog through the house and onto the porch, is palpable. I feel her halt just behind me and glance back to see her scanning the yard in confusion.

There's no car.

A question forms on her lips and I cut it off with a motion toward the yard. "Go."

Her brow wrinkles. "Just…go?"

I nod. "That's right." I glance at my watch and press a button on its side. "I'll even give you a sixty second head start."

Comprehension glares in the fearful roll of her eyes toward the yard and the trees beyond, and she inhales a deep breath. Then she's moving, as quickly, I warrant, as she's able, descending the porch steps and fleeing with stumbling steps into the forest.

I watch her go. Nearly a minute later, my watch beeps. I shut the alarm off and slide the syringe from my pocket. An easy death for this one, a swift fade into eternal slumber. I have no desire to make her suffer.

I step off the porch and walk toward where I saw her enter the woods, knowing I should probably embrace the potential for surprise and select a different entrance point. My brother was always the hunter, though. It was he who truly reveled in this game.

I just want it over with, so I can move on to Shiloh.

The true queen.

10
Shiloh

SCENERY BLURS OUTSIDE THE CAR WINDOW AS I MAKE THE HOUR-LONG DRIVE TO THURSTON HOUSE. I have an appointment to visit Sammy and talk to Dr. Adams about his progression. I'm hoping that he'll release him into my care before too much longer, but I don't know. Sammy is still not walking on his own for any extended time or distance.

Before I left, I grabbed my camera bag in case I decide to take any photos while I'm there, tossing it into the passenger seat. It's been forever since I've taken any photos and Thurston House has a great nature preserve for its residents that I love exploring on pretty days.

I've been thinking more and more about doing something with my photography. I started an Instagram, naming it "Day in the Life." My first photo was a donut I was about to eat, a plump Boston crème oozing creamy filling.

Leaves still cling to a few trees, but for the most part, bare limbs claw their way toward a dull pearl sky. It's an easy drive, and I lose myself in my thoughts as the road unwinds before me like a gunmetal ribbon.

In the rearview mirror, I see a motorcycle following just far enough behind me that I wouldn't notice if I wasn't looking for it. Brodie.

He's stuck to me like a burr ever since the night at Karli's. I tried to reassure him that it was fine—I understood why he was a few minutes behind me instead of right there once he explained. I think he's been kicking his own ass ever since, though, and when Gunner is not around, he refuses to let me out of his sight.

Seeing him in the rearview now, knowing he's watching over me when Gunner can't, is a comfort, now. Gunner's at school today. He has to be careful about the number of days that he misses, especially since he took the day after his accident off only a week or so ago, going with Leila and me to check into the club's client records.

Thurston House appears up ahead. Shaking my head loose of the disturbing thoughts, I pull in and head toward the visitor lot. Seeing Dr. Adams walking with a nurse and a patient on one of the nearby paths, I wave as I climb out of my car, pausing when he breaks away from his companions to jog over to me.

"Shiloh, hi. Is it already time for Sammy's appointment? I lost track of time."

"Oh, no, I'm probably early. I had a little extra time on my hands this morning and thought I would drop in and see Sammy. Maybe see if you had a few minutes to talk about his plan for homecoming?" I shift my camera from my neck to my shoulder and his eyes follow.

"Nice camera you have there."

"Thanks. I've been trying to dig back into my photography lately, maybe do something with it."

"You're interested in photography?"

"It was actually my first choice of major. I changed it after the accident…figured I wouldn't be able to earn enough of a stable income to take care of Sammy."

Dr. Adams lifts an eyebrow. "That's…do you know how many people have that kind of selfless nature, Shiloh?"

"Oh, I wouldn't call it that. I'm not going to lie—there were days when I just wanted to leave. Hop on a plane and fly somewhere sunny. Join the military. Let the state handle it. But I couldn't. He's my brother. We didn't have anyone else, you know?"

"I have a brother. We're pretty close, but I can't imagine him doing something like that for me."

"Would you do it for him?"

He tilts his head. "No. I'm not certain that I would."

I fiddle with my camera and hasten to exit the conversation. "Do you think Sammy would be up to coming out on the nature paths with me today? I thought I might take a few pictures."

"Tell you what. I'll come along with you—" Protesting, I interrupt, but Dr. Adams talks over my objections. "It's no problem at all. I'll enjoy the change of scenery and we can chat about his progress while we walk. Wait here and we'll be out in a few minutes."

True to his word, several minutes later Dr. Adams returns, pushing Sammy in his wheelchair. Sammy sticks his hand up in salute, a grin breaking out over his face. When he gets closer, he peers around. "Where's Gunner? I thought maybe he'd come back."

"He's at school right now, but don't worry, Sam. He'll be back. I'm tutoring him this afternoon, so I'll tell him you said hey." Sammy nods, and we start walking. The preserve starts around fifty yards away from the main house, where a brick pathway fades into a pebbled trail that winds through a dim forest. It's populated heavily with evergreen, so even at this time of year it's verdant and rich with growth, the green canopy of the pines mixing with the spidery branches of their deciduous counterparts. Dr. Adams helps Sammy maneuver his chair over the pebbled path, his arms straining against the fabric of his sweater.

"You're a tutor?" he asks, inclining his head toward me.

"I—yes," I answer, deciding to keep my response brief. He doesn't need to know about Gunner's dyslexia. "English, mainly, but I help with other subjects, as well." We walk further, and by degrees peace seeps into me. "It's so beautiful here."

Sammy murmurs agreement.

"This was part of my family's land," Dr. Adams reveals, catching my attention. "It was in our family for generations, until my mother inherited and decided to sell to the group that funded Thurston House."

"That's kind of crazy," I reply. "I had no idea. Why did she want to sell?"

He shrugs. "It's not common knowledge. She was very philanthropic, felt it could be put to better use than just a family home."

I nod, wondering how he had felt about that, but not wanting to ask.

"So, did you grow up in the house?" Sammy gestures back the way we came.

"I did, yes. It was all very 'high society.'" His eyes are distant as he recalls his past. "My mother had garden parties and ladies' luncheons and even a ball or two."

"Oh, my goodness. That sounds like fun."

This time the look he sends my way is self-deprecating. "Not really. My mother liked to parade her children around, put us on display for her guests." He gives a short laugh. "She actually put us in short pants when we were children. They were obnoxious when I all wanted to do was go jump in the lake."

I snicker. "I bet." We fall silent, and I snap a few shots to retreat gracefully from the conversation. It's too personal, like he's speaking to a friend. While I like Dr. Adams, I don't consider myself a friend. There's too much potential for awkwardness, given his responsibility to my brother.

"Give me a sec," I ask, and lay prone on the ground. From the corner of my eye I see the doctor looking on in confusion as I aim my lens at the sheltering branches above us. I have to get the perspective exactly right, get just those tiny windows of sky peeking through the needles and branches to achieve that mystical feeling I get every time I walk in a place like this. Maybe I'll call it 'windows to heaven,' I think. Or something shorter, simpler. Windows.

"Shiloh, what—"

"Just a minute, doctor. This is what Shiloh calls 'seeing a story,'" I hear Sammy explaining to him. "It can be really annoying, but you just gotta let her do her thing."

"What's that?"

"That's what she calls it when she sees something that she needs to capture and tell—only in a photograph instead of words. You just need to give her a minute to get it right." His words warm me. Sammy always did understand me, more than Mom or anyone else except maybe Cotton.

"Oh. Well, all right."

Image captured, I rise as gracefully as possible to my feet and look around. We've walked relatively deep into the woods, but the path is still level and well-designed, curling through and blending with the forest. The underbrush slopes gently away from it, rolling down into pockets of dense growth broken up by needle-covered circles around the trees. Through them, there's a glint of silvery-blue and I point.

"Is that the lake you were talking about?"

"It is. Would you like to see it?" I nod, and we continue on. I've never been this far back into the preserve before. "So, who is this Gunner fellow, anyway? Did I hear you say he was in school?"

Eyeing him, I debate how to answer. It was obvious when we were here last that there was some tension between the two men. I don't want to give Dr. Adams the wrong impression, but neither do I want to mislead him into thinking there is any hope for anything personal between us. I've never been interested in him that way. Sammy saves me from answering. "He's one of my best friends," he says. "He was pretty much part of our family." He lapses into silence, no doubt remembering the ball games, sleepovers, and camping trips that marked their childhood.

"Ah. For a while there I thought maybe you guys were involved. Romantically, I mean." He presses, a curious gleam in his eye. "But that wouldn't be the case if he's Sammy's age and a student."

"Oh, he's not my age," Sammy says. "He's actually nineteen. He was held back in kindergarten, so he's always been a year older than the rest of us."

I arch a brow at the doctor's nonplussed expression but refrain from commenting and change the subject, instead. It's none of his business. "So, tell me about Sammy's physical therapy needs once he's home."

Adjusting his expression, Dr. Adams accepts the change in topic. "He'll basically require a pretty high-tech home gym set-up…"

I scramble in my bag for a pen and paper, but he assures me with a wave of his hand that he'll send all the information to me in an email, so I relax and simply listen, pausing ever so often to frame another photo. Sammy listens, as well, serious for once as he focuses on the work he will have to do as he continues to retrain and develop his muscles.

Therapy will be two hours every other day, plus one hour on the alternating days for varying muscle groups impacted by the brain and spinal injury. The two-hour group will focus on Sammy's legs, which he is just beginning to regain some control over but are still exhibiting immense weakness and lack of coordination. While those areas should improve considerably in the coming weeks, we will need to continue his treatment once he is home in order to ensure his muscles continue to improve.

We'll also work in therapy in fine motor skills, cognitive, and speech therapy. A visiting therapist will assist with all of this, thank goodness, and the residence facility's goal in the coming weeks will be to get Sammy to a point of independence. They want him to be capable of showering on his own, making his own meals, and essentially looking out for his own comfort if left to his own devices for any length of time. Sammy nods, all of this sounding appealing as far as I can tell from his expression.

It sounds great, but I have to ask the question that's been haunting me since around midway into Dr. Adams's explanation. "All of this sounds expensive.

Any ideas how much it will cost, or if insurance will cover it?"

"Maybe I can get some kind of job, sis?" Sammy asks.

I stop on the path, stunned. "Sam, that isn't…I didn't mean…"

Dr. Adams stops the wheelchair and takes my elbow. "Let's not talk about how much the cost will be right now, hmm?"

I walk a short distance away, Dr. Adams strolling after me. The path we're walking opens up, and before us stretches a small lake, manmade judging by its perfect oval shape. Across the expanse of water, there's a small cabin with a covered porch. "Fishing cabin?" I guess, arching a brow. He nods assent and places his hands in his pockets. "It's so pretty." I take a few photos. "Quiet. Peaceful."

"Yes, it's one of my favorite places. Regarding the financials, I don't think you'll need to worry too much, Shiloh," he says. "I'm sure insurance will cover most of it."

Chewing my lip, I admit, "I'll need to check on my insurance. I kind of resigned recently from my teaching position."

One well-shaped eyebrow arches. "Oh?"

"What the hell, Shiloh?" Sammy hadn't looked to be paying attention to our conversation, but I guess he was. I grimace and wave the unasked question away. "Long story."

"I'm a good listener." It's Dr. Adams that speaks.

"I really don't want to talk about it, but thanks." Sammy looks at me and I avert my gaze, giving him a subtle flick of the wrist. *I'll talk to you later,* it promises.

I turn back toward the path. "You guys ready? Oh, wait. What are those?" There are several interesting little hillocks several yards off the path, each covered in fungi.

Dr. Adams shrugs. "Just a ground formation, I suppose." He steps closer, and to my surprise, he places a hand on my shoulders, a thumb brushing softly against my clavicle. My smile slips and I try to shuffle backwards, but his hand tightens. "Don't worry, Shiloh. Whatever isn't covered, you have friends. Friends who care about you and Sammy very much." I look past him, to Sammy, who's staring with ill-concealed interest.

"Dr. Adams," I pause, take a breath. "I'm not sure where you're going with this—" He smiles down at me and starts to speak, and I'm forced to confront the fact that he does not have neutral feelings toward me.

"I'm not going anywhere at all with it, except to remind you that everyone loves you guys here, Shiloh. Your brother is a special part of Thurston House. Our staff—they are always talking about the goodies you bring each weekend. There's no reason at all to worry about Sammy's care. We'll make sure he's taken care of. Okay?"

"Umm…okay, I guess."

"I could probably even wrangle you a job here at Thurston House. We have several younger patients who are still in school. I don't think an in-house tutor is a far-fetched idea."

"Really?" I blink at him, surprised. "That's…incredibly generous."

"Not at all. You'd be filling a need. Let me talk about it with our board and I'll let you know their thoughts."

"Thank you." I shake my head a little, unclear how we got to this point. A private teaching position…it would be a solution to this predicament I found myself in.

He doesn't release my shoulder, and for a second, I get the impression he intends to kiss me. He's leaning in, his eyes focused on my mouth, every muscle of his body intent in a single direction. Shocked, I pull back sharply out of his grasp.

"What are you doing?"

As I jerk away, I step back on the edge of the rocky path, which slopes down into the mossy undergrowth of the forest. My ankle catches on a rock, twisting, and down I go, rolling in an undignified heap all the way down the hill as I try to protect my camera rather than break my fall.

Crying out as I fall, I hear Sammy's exclamation. "Shy!" Underbrush stabs and pokes at me and I wince as I roll over and sit up, brushing the detritus from my legs. More dirt and grit comes rolling down at me as Dr. Adams slides down to me, arms held out for balance on the steep hillside.

"Shiloh, are you okay?" His hands are under my armpits, helping me rise, and I wince as I try to put my weight on my ankle. It's a definite sprain.

"My ankle," I tell him, allowing him to help me up the hill and pulling away when we reach the top. "Pretty sure I've sprained or twisted it." Sammy makes a sound of distress and I look at him with apology. "Sorry, Sam. I stepped wrong." I toss him my phone. "Do me a favor and text Brodie? He's in my contacts. It's my right ankle so I'm going to need a ride and Gunner's in school."

"Who's Brodie?" Sammy asks, searching my contacts.

Shit. Me and my big mouth. "Ah...he's a friend," I tell him. I don't want him to know I have a stalker.

"I'll be happy to drive you back, Shiloh," Dr. Adams offers.

"No, that's okay. Thank you, anyway."

"If you're certain. I'll need you to fill out an accident report while you wait if you don't mind. We'll get you some ice when we get back, too..."

I accept the elbow he offers as support to limp back to the main residence and eye him warily, trying to ignore the shafts of pain spearing through my ankle as we move along the path. Should I bring it up? Was I imagining things? He seems so normal now, so professional, but surely, I'm not completely crazy. There was that glint in his eye, his head moving closer to my own...Shaking my head, I decide I must have been mistaken, letting my paranoia get to me.

Nausea roils in me at the thought of continuing under this umbrella of fear for even another minute. It infiltrates everything, makes me question everyone's smallest move or word. I'm second-guessing and attaching motives to things I normally wouldn't think twice about, and I can't stand it. This isn't me, this suspicious person who eyes everyone with distrust.

"Shiloh? Hanging in there?" Dr. Adams places a hand at my hip and provides even more assistance, fair lifting me in spots so I don't put weight on my ankle. I've never noticed before how strong he is, but I guess it makes sense, considering his practice is in rehabilitation and physical therapy.

I smile for Sammy's sake, seeing him glance back at us. "I'm fine. Just ready to sit down, I guess."

"Almost there." We're on the brick paved path now, and after a brief hesitation he speaks again. "Look...I don't usually do this, but I just wanted you to know that I think you're pretty special."

"Oh. Dr. Adams—"

"Jason," he corrects.

"I think we need to keep this professional."

"Professional."

"Yes. You're my brother's doctor. I think it best."

He dips his head and I feel his fingers on my waist clench before he loosens them. "You're right, of course." Pause. "So, it's not that you're not attracted to me?" Inwardly I roll my eyes at the preciousness of the male ego.

"Not at all! You're a keeper, Dr. Adams." I try to nudge him playfully without losing my balance. He looks so crestfallen. "Any girl would be lucky to have you."

"But not you."

"I would just really prefer to keep things professional," I say again. "I'm not looking for a relationship right now, anyway."

He sighs. "I understand."

We're quiet for a while, and the silence feels broody. "Still friends?"

The smile he sends me is blinding. "Of course, we're still friends. Professional ones. Ah, here we are." The forest ends, Thurston House sitting just across the lawn from us.

When we reach the main house, I drop onto a bench on the wide, covered porch that spans the width of the building, immediately raising my leg up to counteract the swelling I can already feel. Sammy pulls his chair alongside me.

"Can you get what she needs, Dr. Adams?" he asks. "If I know Shiloh, she won't go to the doctor."

"Of course." Dr. Adams disappears inside and I look up into Sammy's dark expression.

"It's all right, Sam. It's not like I haven't done this half a dozen times before, dancing. I even have a boot at home."

"What happened out there, Shy? And don't tell me you tripped."

I shrug. "I honestly don't know how to answer that, Sammy. I got a little skeeved, is all. It looked like he might have been moving in for a kiss, but I think it was my imagination."

"You don't have an imagination."

"Ha, ha."

"Do I need to talk to him?"

"No! Oh, my gosh, no. I just told him I was not interested in him and he seemed to be fine with it. Just let it go. Maybe he has a crush. Embarrassing the man won't accomplish anything."

Sammy looks at me hard for a long minute, and then we lapse into silence until it's broken by Dr. Adams's arrival with an ice pack. He hands me that and a scrip for a painkiller, which I tuck into my pocket.

"Thanks, doc."

"Certainly. Well, listen, I need to get back to work. I'll leave Sammy out here with you until your ride arrives, and if you don't mind making sure he gets back to his room before you leave…?"

"Of course."

"Great. And Shelby has an accident report at the front desk—I explained everything, and she's already typed it up for you. Just give it a read, make any alterations you wish, and sign if it looks good."

"That sounds great. Thank you, again."

With a wave, he goes back inside, leaving Sammy and me alone once again. We sit quietly with our separate thoughts until Brodie arrives, his bike a throttled roar as he pulls to a stop in the parking lot. He had probably been waiting just down the drive for me to emerge. Sammy looks at me askance.

"Don't tell me you're getting on that thing with your ankle messed up?"

"No, Dad." Brodie comes strolling up and I offer him a brief wave as I stand. "He'll have to leave it here. Brodie, this is my brother, Sammy. Sammy, Brodie. Brodie's a friend of Gunner."

The two men do that weird handshake, hand clasp thing and Brodie looks my way.

"You ready?" He commandeers my camera and slings it carefully around his neck and beneath his arm.

"Yup." I give Sammy a hug and allow Brodie to help me down the steps and to my car.

"Gunner's going to want a report."

"I'm well aware. It was nothing serious. Just me being clumsy."

Brodie considers as he helps me into the passenger seat, his eyes narrowed. "Hmm. Something you're not is clumsy, Shiloh."

I shrug. "First time for everything, I guess."

11
Gunner

LIFTING MY DRINK—soda tonight, no alcohol—I lean back into the padded seat and survey the scene around me. Kendrick's is dead tonight, with the exception of a group of frat guys having some kind of celebration near the main stage. It may be because it's Sunday and cold as fuck outside.

Shiloh's been back for just a little over a week now, tending bar in a sexy tuxedo-style get-up that at least covers all of the important bits. She's wearing a clunk black boot over her pants, but no sees it with her tucked behind the bar the way she is. It reminds me that I need to talk to her about whatever happened at Thurston House yesterday.

I don't want to bring it up, though. She's so much more relaxed than I've ever seen her, actually smiling and laughing with the customers and the senior bartender, some guy named Teddy.

He's good at keeping his eyes to himself, which makes me like him all right. Not just where Shiloh is concerned, either. He's coolly professional with all of the women that work here, keeping his gaze disinterested and above the neck.

I'm not seeing anyone, really, who shows that kind of interest in Shiloh. No one who stands out, no cause for alarm in anyone the entire week she's been back. And I've been here watching every single shift, driving her to work over her protests, sitting in this same booth where I have a sweeping view of the club, and driving her back home again at the end of her shift.

Brodie has continued to watch at night, and nothing's happened there, either.

It's making me nervous. There's no way Shiloh's stalker has just given up and gone away. He's too obsessed; he's already shown that hand. No, the fucker is smart, and he's biding his time.

Irritated, I throw some cash down on the table for a tip and get up, making my way toward the bar. Shiloh has another fifteen minutes on shift and then we'll be out of here.

It's probably not smart of me to sit here during all of her shifts like a lovesick puppy, but I can't help myself. Leaving her alone is not an option, not until we catch this guy.

Choosing a stool on her end of the bar, I slide onto it and wait while she finishes up with a customer.

"Psst."

"Psst, yourself." She wipes at a ring of moisture on the bar top before her.

"What are you doing this week?"

"Not enough. I'm not on schedule after today. Danny said they're slow this week, so I'm not needed. We're closed for Thanksgiving, not reopening until Saturday." Finished cleaning, she rests both hands on the edge of the bar on either side of her and observes me. "Why?"

"We always go out of town this week, spend the holiday at our cabin in Massanutten. Do some skiing, weather permitting. Be lazy, eat lots of junk."

Shiloh busies herself putting away clean glassware. "That sounds like fun."

"It is. Relaxing, but nice. Thanksgiving is Esme's birthday, so it's something we started doing after Mom died. Dad told me once that we needed to attach some other meaning and memory to the holiday and Esme's birthday, other than mom's death."

"That's...that's so wise of him, Gunner." She falls silent, thinking, no doubt, of her own mother's death at a different holiday—Christmas Eve. I resolve to help her attach some different significance to it this year, and all the years that follow, if she'll let me.

God, I'm whipped.

Shiloh's speaking and I whip my attention back to her. "...hadn't realized your and Esme's birthdays were so close together. When is yours, anyway? Isn't it November or December?"

I fidget with a stack of square cardboard coasters on the bar in front of me. "Ah...it was yesterday, actually."

Shiloh stops moving. "Your birthday was yesterday?"

I nod, tugging my hat a bit lower over my eyes.

"And you didn't tell me...why?"

"Because it wasn't a big deal." She narrows her eyes at me. "I'm not five, Shiloh. I don't need a party and presents."

"Maybe I would have liked to have said, 'hey. Glad you were born.'" She huffs out a breath. "That's what birthdays are about. Not presents. I might even have made you a cake."

"Well, damn. I definitely should have said something." I pause and clear my throat. "So, how about it?"

Her forehead crinkles. "How about what?"

"Come with us!" I think back and realize I hadn't actually asked her—just told her we were going.

"I can't. Hang on a sec." Shiloh walks over to Teddy and exchanges a few words, then returns, bending to grab her purse from under the bar. "I'm done. Let's go."

We pause for Shiloh to slip into her coat, hanging on a hook in the back, and then we head out the employee door to the parking lot.

The first few snowflakes of the season are drifting down in slow motion, and Shiloh stops to hold her bare hands out, her face turned up to the sky in awe.

"It's snowing!" she exclaims the obvious and pokes out her tongue.

I laugh. "You are such a little kid." Birthday cake and snow.

"When it comes to snow, I hope I never grow up. Ah, I hope it gets deep. I love to sit beside the window and just stare out at it." Her expression is dreamy. "All the dirty browns and grays of winter covered in this pristine coat of white snow paint." It's melting on her glasses, little dots of water that hide her eyes from me. I take them off and clean them carefully with my handkerchief before bundling her into the farm truck that I'm using now that mine is in the garage being repaired. "C'mon, you nut."

I crank up the heat and ease carefully out of the lot and onto the road that'll take us home. The snow is already starting to stick a little, although I don't think it's expected to do much. It's still too early in the season. We tend to get a lot in the higher elevations, both earlier and later in the season than other nearby locations.

"Back to this week." I speak into the swoosh of the windshield wipers disturbing the otherwise quiet cab. "Why can't you come?"

"I can't bust in on your family like that, Gunner. It's Esme's birthday. And Thanksgiving."

"And you're not going to spend it alone."

"I won't—I usually visit Sammy. The cafeteria there will have some turkey and dressing."

I shake my head. "Shiloh, if you don't come with us, I'm staying here. It's not only the holiday. There's been nothing out of this guy for over a week now. I don't like it. It's like he's waiting for something."

She shrinks further into her coat. "I've been hoping he was gone."

"I don't want to scare you, but I don't think we're going to get that lucky."

She sighs. "You're probably right. But I still can't leave Sammy alone on Thanksgiving while I go hang out with your family. It wouldn't be right."

"Fine. I'm staying. We'll go see Sammy together Thanksgiving Day, bring the feast to him."

"Gunner, no! Your dad needs you."

I focus on the road beyond the windshield, the snow coming down thicker now and lessening visibility. I'm reminded of my accident not too long ago. Rain and a shattered windshield were the culprits then, but it still messes with my nerves. "I'll talk to him, Shiloh. Don't worry about that." She's about to argue and I take a hand off the wheel to halt the words. "And there's Brodie, Shy. I'd like to give the man some time off." With an indistinct growl, she crosses her arms over her chest and subsides. I knew that argument would do what all the begging wouldn't. I stifle a grin and continue. "We'll go shopping tomorrow, get a turkey. And a pumpkin pie."

"If there are any turkeys left the Monday before Thanksgiving," she grumbles. "I don't think I even know how to cook a turkey."

"Guess we'll figure that out together." Reaching over, I pull her left hand into mine. "It's settled."

12
Shiloh

SNOW LAYERS THE LANDSCAPE IN A COAT SEVERAL INCHES THICK when Gunner arrives a few minutes past nine the next morning. The previous evening's storm is past, leaving the sun shining with a painful glare off the white.

Hearing Gunner's boots on the porch as he stomps snow from their soles, I open the door to let him in, trying to ignore the flutter in my stomach.

"Morning." He flashes a smile that shows off that chin dimple, leans in to press a cold kiss upon my cheek, and brushes past me into the foyer. The ease of it is unsettling, and inwardly I mock myself for how easily I abandoned any pretense of space between us—not all at once, but inch by inch, one tiny concession at a time. How could I not? When Gunner wants something he's like the drip of water on stone.

I shut the door and help tug his jacket off, hanging it afterward on one of the hooks by the door. As he bends to pull his wet shoes off, I make my way into the kitchen.

"Coffee?"

He follows me on socked feet. "Gross, no. You have a soda?" Making himself at home, he opens the fridge and peers inside. "Jackpot." He grabs a Coke and pops the tab, drinking deeply. "So, what's on the agenda for today?"

Leaning against the counter, I take a sip of my coffee. "You mentioned something about grocery shopping?

And I know this isn't terribly exciting, but I always put a Christmas tree up this week."

"Sounds fun," he responds. "Real or fake?"

"I have allergies," I tell him. "I love a real tree, but they literally make me sick. So fake for me, unfortunately."

"Ours is fake for the same reason. Esme has terrible allergies to anything green." He shakes his head. "Sucks to be her. You have one here?" When I nod, he continues. "I'll pull it out later." He sets his drink down on the counter and prowls my way. "Right now, I want to kiss my hot girlfriend."

There's a lightness in my chest at his words, and I only barely manage to set my mug down before he's on me, one finger tilting my chin up, pale gray-blue eyes focused intently on mine.

For some reason, I'm nervous. We've kissed before, but it feels different now. Less like something stolen, and more like a promise. Like we're on the cusp of something.

Gunner moves his finger and cups my jaw with both hands, and as I wait without breathing, he slides them down my neck and to my shoulders. We're not touching anywhere else and yet I'm suffused with heat. With expectation.

"Is that okay?" he asks.

"If you kiss me? Or that you called me your girlfriend?"

"Either. Both."

"Yes."

"Good answer." He dips his head and then stops, his lips a scant breath from mine. His eyes, so close to mine, are hooded as he lets the seconds stretch by, ratcheting up the anticipation strung tight between us. My tongue darts out to wet my lips, a clear signal that I'm ready, but he either doesn't notice or chooses to ignore me. *Tease.* I try again, tilting my head the tiniest bit and leaning forward to get things moving. His mouth curves in a grin as he leans back in response.

I narrow my eyes. "Kiss me, damnit."

His eyes crinkle at the corners, and he cancels the inches between our lips, slanting his mouth over mine with strokes that sip and tempt. His hands make a slow slide down to my waist and he lifts me, easily enough to impress and make me swoon a little as he sets me on the countertop behind us. He steps between my legs, hands still at my waist.

His lips travel to nip at my jawline and then down my neck, where he sucks gently.

I drop my head back, giving him more room, and notice that I'm shaking. Full out shaking, and from a kiss.

My hands are still gripping the edge of the countertop. I move them to Gunner's shoulders, and then his chest. It's firm beneath my palms, the muscles flexing at my touch. His own hands are moving— stroking, soothing, inciting, urging every part he can reach—and as a big hand covers my breast, that area of my brain that clings to reason knows we need to stop before we reach the point where we can't.

"Gunner," I whisper.

His lips abandon the collarbone they are currently exploring and return to my mouth. Silencing me.

I grasp his head, wind my fingers through his inky hair, and yank him away after pressing a final hard kiss to his mouth. "We need to stop."

Those winter eyes are unfocused as he stares. He blinks and I see awareness return. The hands at my waist bite momentarily into my flesh and then his thumbs soothe the area.

"Stop." He drops his face into the crook of my neck and inhales deeply. "Yeah. Okay, give me a minute."

We hold each other loosely as I give him his minute, both of us breathing heavily. Then slowly, reluctantly, he sets me back down on the floor and steps away.

"I'm sorry," I say.

He frowns. "For what?"

"For letting things go that far and then slamming on the brakes."

Gunner eyes me curiously. "Babe, I don't know who you've been dating, but one—that was a kiss. A hot one, yeah, but a kiss. I didn't even get your shirt off." His lips crook in wry humor. "Although I might've thought about it. And two—it doesn't matter how far things have gone. Whether it's just a kiss or if my dick is ready to slide home—" I wince at the expression and he smirks. "—it's never too late to stop." He touches my cheek with one finger. "Whoever told you there's a point where you can't is a douche."

I look away. *Tell him!* My brain screams. Things are moving inexorably in one direction, and I know as well as I know my own name: we're going to end up in bed together.

Gunner is going to be my first.

The thought settles, solidifies, takes shape and meaning. Strangely, I'm not as panicked by the idea as I once was. It feels right. Like he said, we've been moving in this direction since he was ten and I was thirteen.

I'd just closed my mind to it.

But he needs to know.

"Hey." He chucks me under the chin, making my eyes flicker to his and then away again. "What's going on in that beautiful head of yours?"

"A lot," I answer honestly. Is he one of those guys who get freaked out by virgins? Will he consider my virginity a burden or a gift? Maybe, as wrong and weird as the idea feels—maybe this will be the thing that makes him run.

"Shiloh?" He presses back into me at the counter. "Look at me." Reluctant, I meet his eyes. "You're starting to worry me. Did someone—" He stops and swallows, and his meaning hits me.

"No! God, no. Nothing like that." Now or never. I take in a deep breath, release it. "I'm a virgin." *There. I said it.* I cover my face with my hands, peek at him through two fingers. He doesn't say anything; just stares at me. "I've never done this before," I add for good measure.

"Oh." Finally, he speaks. "I wasn't expecting that, but okay."

Annoyance pokes at me like my brother used to do when he wanted attention. I didn't expect a parade, but *okay*? That's underwhelming. "What were you expecting, out of curiosity?"

"Just…not that. I mean, it's fine. It's great. Definitely not a problem. But I wouldn't have guessed it. You worked in a strip club, you know?"

"So, that must mean I have loads of experience." He winces at my sarcasm but refuses to move when I shove at him. "Move."

"No." He lifts me up and sets me back in my spot on the counter. "That's not what I meant. I just meant…you're really fucking good at turning guys on, Shiloh. Especially considering your overall lack of experience." He grins at me. "It's impressive."

I roll my eyes. "It's whatever. I'm a dancer, Gunner. I learned how to use my body a long time ago."

He nods, and I wonder if he even realizes his hands are stroking up and down the sides of my thighs. I shiver. "Anyway. I just wanted you to know, in case…just in case," I finish.

He nods again and dips his head to place a whisper-light kiss on my mouth. "I'm glad you told me. I'll be careful with you."

He steps back, setting me down on the floor once again and running a hand through his hair. "So. Groceries first?"

GETTING GROCERIES WITH GUNNER IS ODDLY FUN. He's an overgrown kid in many ways, standing on the bottom of the cart and popping a wheelie before propelling it down an empty aisle. Juggling apples—terribly. Opening a pack of cookies and munching on them as we strolled through the store.

He makes me smile, during a time when I have very little to smile about. It's hard to discount that.

We manage to find a turkey, and as we remember things we want to eat we traverse back and forth to toss items into the cart. Potatoes. Green beans. Dressing mix. Marshmallows for the sweet potatoes.

"Gunner." I stop him at the end of the baking aisle. "How are we going to eat all of this? Just the two of us?"

He smirks at me. "Never fear. I have a pretty obnoxious appetite, but I can always call Miles. And we're taking some to Sammy, too."

"Oh, that's true." I shook my head. I had forgotten about taking the meal to Sammy. What kind of sister was I? We start walking again, heading to the dairy section for milk and eggs.

"Do you know that guy?" Gunner indicates a man standing a fair distance away. He's staring at us and I squint, trying to figure out who he is without making it obvious.

"That's Mark Lincoln, I think. He dated my mom for a while before the accident."

Gunner whipped his head back to me. "Mark Lincoln, the one that's a member of Kendricks?"

"One and the same." I offer a small wave to him, not knowing what else to do, and he starts toward us.

"Interesting."

"Shiloh." Lincoln stops a few feet away. "How have you been doing? It's been a while."

How long is a while, I wonder. Two years or two weeks? "I've been doing pretty good, Mark. Keeping busy. How about you?"

"Same old, same old. I sold the shop not too long ago."

"Really? Why?" I'm surprised. Mark had run an outdoorsman supply business that had been in his family for several generations. It catered to fishermen, hunters, campers, hikers, and even bikers, selling outdoor supplies and renting cabins. From what Mom had told me, it was a business that did very well.

"I was just tired. I'd been working there since I was a kid. Thirty years, you know? I was close to retirement but didn't have a clue what to do with it." I nod. Mark didn't have kids, no logical person to move into an owner-operator role. "So, when I got an offer, I snapped at it."

"What are you doing now?"

He leans in closer, an amused glint in his eyes. "That's just it. I don't have to do anything now. Nor ever again, if I don't want to. Not to be crass, but the buyout was huge. It's pretty awesome."

"That's great, Mark. I'm happy for you."

"So, what are you doing? And how's Sammy?"

I take my time answering, reaching down to check the cartons of eggs for broken ones. How to say, *well, I was a stripper. Maybe you saw me?* "Not much at the minute. Just stopped teaching. I'm doing some tutoring and trying to figure out what I really want to do. I'm thinking about getting back into my photography. I've been playing around with that again."

"You were always so good at that."

"Sammy's good. He may be able to come home soon."

"I'm so glad to hear that! I've worried about him, about you." He looks at the floor and he suddenly looks tired, the lines on his face deep grooves compared to the man I remember.

The man I remember stopping by to pick Mom up was youthful looking for his age, which I recall being close to fifty. His face was lightly tanned, with fine white lines crinkling the corners of his eyes from squinting into the sun. His body looked younger than his age, as well, trim and fairly muscular.

He's not unrecognizable now, but he has aged in the past few years, putting on a little weight and settling more comfortably into his middle years.

I tell him thank you, and notice his eyes flicking past me to Gunner, who to this point has been a silent observer.

"Oh, sorry. Gunner, Mark Lincoln. Mark, Gunner Ford." They reach past me to shake each other's hands and I finish lamely, "My friend." Gunner slants me a look and I wince, then shrug. *Sorry,* my shrug says. *I panicked a little.*

You're going to pay for that, his eyes return.

If Mark clues into the silent exchange between us, he gives no sign. He smiles genially and he and Gunner chat briefly about some kind of camping gear while I look around the store and mentally check off our list. It's nice to see Mark and doing so makes me feel better about his club membership, but I'm starting to feel antsy and want to move on. While I'm reassured after a few minutes' conversation that there's no way he's my stalker, I don't like revisiting the past.

"Mark, it was really great to see you. We have somewhere to be, so we're going to get moving," I lie. Gunner eyes me again but doesn't rat me out.

After a hug and a promise "not to be a stranger," we move on, walking a few steps down the aisle to grab a jug of milk before turning toward the front of the store.

"In a hurry?" Gunner asks.

"Not really. It was just getting awkward." I glance at him as he pushes the cart slowly up the aisle. "Good news, though—I don't think he's the guy."

"What makes you say that?"

I lift one shoulder and let it fall. "Nothing concrete. Just a sense...I don't know. I feel okay around him. I get a dad, or a favorite uncle vibe." I brush my hair out of my face and wind it into a loose knot at the nape of my neck. "Does that make any sense?"

"Of course." At the register we start unloading the cart onto the belt. "Maybe we need to focus on anyone who's made you feel less than okay...look at instinct for a little while."

"Hmmm." I tap a finger to my bottom lip." I'll have to think about that."

We close the subject as the cashier rings everything up, and Gunner pulls out a card to pay. I'd like to protest, but knowing it's useless, refrain, and we finish up quickly.

Truck loaded up with groceries that cover the back seat and spill over into the floorboard, we start for home. Or at least, my home. Strange considering how early it is yet, but I've already started thinking about things in terms of one half of a couple. This isn't *my* Thanksgiving holiday...it's *ours*. Those groceries aren't for *my* Thanksgiving meal, but one for *us*. It's not what *I* need to do, but what are *we* doing.

"So..." Gunner's voice breaks into my thoughts. "Any ideas?"

It takes me a minute to realize what he's referring to. "Anyone who makes me feel uncomfortable?" I ask to be sure, and he nods, pulling the truck into the drive thru of our Dairy Queen.

"This okay? I know it's not filet mignon, but I kind of have a craving."

I smile across at him. "I don't need filet, Gunner. I would love a chili cheese dog right now..." I lick my lips, thinking about it. "And a milkshake, please." I fall quiet while he gives our order. "Oh! Onion rings, too."

When he side-eyes me I shrug. "I haven't eaten here in forever."

After we have our food and start pulling away, I return to the earlier conversation. "There's one, maybe two people I can think of who occasionally make me a bit uncomfortable."

"Okay."

"One's Danny."

"At the club?" I nod and Gunner rubs the scruff on his chin and neck. "Hmm. Would he have been able to slip into your peep show unnoticed?"

"I have no idea. It would depend a lot on how busy we were, what kind of traffic we had in the halls. Clients enter and exit, as you know, from the opposite, parallel hall. It's not inconceivable that he could come and go without anyone who works in the club knowing otherwise. We're all on the other side, except for the bouncers who hang out on the client side."

"Right."

We arrive home and Gunner cuts off the truck. "You take lunch in; I'll grab groceries?"

"That works."

While I set our food out on the small kitchen table, Gunner makes short work of hauling the groceries in, carrying what looks to be five or more bags in each hand. He sets them down on the floor and grabs a fry, shoving it in his mouth as he strides back to the door.

"Need any help?"

"I've got it...one more trip." He's gone and back again in moments, the frozen turkey in one arm and more bags in the other. Taking the turkey from him. I set it in the sink, and we sit to eat.

"You said one or two people. Who's the other?" He asks, taking a bite of his hot dog that leaves barely half remaining.

I wipe my hands on the napkin in my lap. "Dr. Adams," I answer.

"Sammy's doctor?" His eyes widen.

"I think it's just me. He's...interested, you know?"

"Oh, I know, all right," Gunner mutters.

I ignore him. "So, I think it's just me being uncomfortable around a guy I'm not interested in, more than anything nefarious—"

Gunner groans and slaps his hand across his chest. "Nefarious, she says. God, Shiloh. Talk nerdy to me."

I punch him in the arm. "Stop it, you weirdo. I'm saying it's just...awkward."

Sobering, Gunner nods thoughtfully. "All right. Good starting points, if nothing else."

"How so?"

Gunner looks at me and there's a resolute firmness to his features that I've never noticed before. "We give their names to Twiggy and let her start digging. If there's anything there, she'll find it."

13

Gunner

AFTER WE EAT, I help Shiloh put away the groceries and then walk out onto the porch to call Twiggy. Maybe I'm being paranoid, but I don't want to take the chance that this guy has managed to reinstall listening devices.

Twiggy is her usual peppy self when she answers. "Talk."

"Hello to you, too."

"All I heard was blah, blah, blah. What's up, G-Man?"

Shaking my head at the name, I answer. "I have a couple of names I'd like you to run for me, see if anything hits or seems off."

"I can do that."

"You ready?"

"Give me a sec."

I hear her rustling about and wait, stamping my feet in the thin coating of snow that has blown on to the porch. I slide my free hand across my chest, under my armpit for warmth. My jacket still hangs on the back of the chair I sat in for lunch and it's cold in my tee shirt, the wind slicing right through the thin cotton.

Dad predicted it would be a cold winter. Judging from the early storm, I'm inclined to agree with him. We skipped straight past first frost into snow. Strangely, though, it could as easily be sixty degrees tomorrow. Virginia weather is just messed up that way. Ever cautious, Dad pruned not too long ago with that in mind, leaving double trunks on each plant when normally he would have pruned them down to a single trunk. The vineyard is all bristly, stalky vines now, rather than the lush green of the summer and early fall.

"'K. I'm ready." Twiggy is back.

"I need you to run Danny Mathis, the manager over at Kendricks. That's M-A—"

Twiggy interrupts me. "I can spell. Who's next?"

"Dr. Adams over at Thurston House. I think his first name is Jason."

"That's going to yield pretty common results. Thurston House should help narrow it down, though. Anyone else?"

I think for a second. Those are the only one Shiloh said gave her an uncomfortable feeling, but what about her ex-boyfriend? "Shane Reasor, too."

"Got it. Okay, give me a day or two and I'll give you a call when I have it ready."

"That works. Call only me, okay? Shiloh knows what I'm doing but I don't want to take a chance that this guy somehow has tracking software on her phone or in her house."

"Nothing wrong with a little caution."

Twiggy disconnects abruptly, without saying good-bye or eff you or anything. It's somewhat par for the course. When Twiggy has something on the brain, she's focused one hundred percent in that direction. She was probably in the middle of something and I interrupted her.

After another quick glance around at the quiet neighborhood, I open the door to step back inside. We have a lot to do today.

MAYBE I'M A SENTIMENTAL IDIOT, but today has been one of the best I've had in a long time. As I finish connecting the last strand of colorful lights on Shiloh's tree and slide out from under it, I can't help the childlike sense of eagerness that grips me.

"Ready to test them out?"

Shiloh's behind me, sorting through a box of ornaments. "Yes! No, wait—let me turn the lights off, first." The light clicks off a moment later, and Shiloh comes to stand beside me.

I drape my arm over her shoulders and pull her into me, the other hand holding the section of cord with the on-off switch. I feel her bounce a little on her toes and look down at her face as I depress the button. I can see the lights in my peripheral, but I don't turn to look at my handiwork. Instead, I want to see Shiloh's expression, illuminated by the twinkling glow.

She's so damn pretty. Her hair, that deep reddish brown, is pulled over one shoulder in a loose braid. Tendrils float around her face, framing clear hazel eyes that shine with catchlights. Excitement is there in the wide grin that stretches her cheeks. A shadow of sadness weakens that smile for a fleeting second before it fades into acceptance. Overall, her face is happy.

She catches me staring and brushes at the hair around her face self-consciously. "What?"

"Nothing." I don't turn away. "You're beautiful."

A blush tints her cheeks, visible even in the dimness, and she clears her throat. Breaking clear of my arm, she turns and pushes the coffee table out of the way, against the couch.

"What are you doing?"

She grabs the throw blanket, a thick crocheted knit, and lays it on the floor. "Didn't you ever lie down on the floor and look at the lights when you were a kid?" While I watch in bemusement, she drops to the floor and grabs my hand, pulling me down with her.

I lie back on the blanket, one hand tucked beneath my head and the other resting on my stomach. Shiloh settles against me, resting her head on the bicep curled at my head and nuzzling into my side. She lays a hand over mine on my stomach and I turn mine palm up, lacing our fingers together.

There, in a room silent save for the susurration of our breaths, we gaze at a ceiling of evergreen and stars.

"Tell me about your absolute favorite Christmas." Shiloh's thumb traces random shapes on my palm as she stares upward, voice sleepy. I consider her question.

"That would probably be when I was around twelve. Dad and Nonna went all out that year. They surprised me with a dog. A retriever."

"You have a dog? I didn't realize."

"He's dead. Hit by a car a few years later."

"Oh, no! That's terrible, Gunner. Way to depress me," she grumbles. "Especially since I've been thinking about getting a dog when Sammy comes home."

"Well, the Christmas was nice, anyway. What kind of dog do you want?"

I feel her shrug against me. "I hadn't gotten that far.

I just know I want something sweet to curl up with and something that'll bark if there's any trouble."

I move the arm under my head and wrap it around her shoulders, pulling her closer to me. "Get something that barks, but you can curl up with me. I'm sweet."

She snickers. "Somehow I had a feeling you were going to say that. You are sweet." Tipping her face up, she places a soft kiss against my jawline.

Which leads to me lowering my face and kissing her. We stay like that, curled into each other and exchanging unhurried, lazy kisses that go no farther than our mouths but are fiercely intimate all the same.

We fall asleep like that, and sometime later I wake slowly, caught for a time between dreams and reality as I work to make sense of my situation.

I'm on the floor, a blanket twisted around my ankles. I've pillowed my head on my arm again, and it's dead asleep. I wince at the thought of the pins and needles that will prickle once I move. Shiloh's curled up into my side, snoring softly. It must be what woke me. It's more really deep breathing than a rumbling snore, but still...

I smile to myself, listening. Shiloh, snoring. It's adorable and I know I'll be teasing her about it as soon as she awakens.

Carefully I ease my arm from beneath Shiloh's head, using my free hand to cup and lower her head to the blanket. I stand and stretch, taking a peek at my watch as I do. Just past midnight. I'll put Shiloh to bed so she doesn't wake stiff as a board tomorrow.

I'm squatting to roll her into my arms when everything goes to hell.

The big picture window where the tree sits just off-center shatters as an object comes hurtling through. It lands with a dull *thunk* on the sofa as glass rains all around us. I cover Shiloh with my body intuitively, shielding her from the worst of it, but she comes up swinging in my arms, knocking me off balance and pushing me down to the floor.

"What's happening?" she screams, eyes darting wildly about to find the threat.

I grunt when she shoves a hand against me as she tries to rise. "Rock or something through the window. Here. This way." I pull her into the kitchen and open the pantry door. "Hide. I'm calling the cops."

"You can't just leave me in here!" she clutches at my shirt. Seeing her phone plugged up on the counter, I grab it and shove it her way. "Here. You call the cops. I need to see if he's still here."

"What? No!"

"Stay here, Shiloh." Giving her a hard look, I shut the door and move back in the direction of the foyer. My shoes are there, and my coat, and I shove my feet in the boots while I'm shrugging into my jacket. I skip tying them and rush outside instead, ignoring the sharp slap of cold that hits me immediately.

There's nothing.

The yard is empty, serene in the pale moonlight. There are no visible footprints, no cars on the street, no puffs of smoke from an idling engine or the glare of taillights disappearing in the distance. From the house on the lot behind Shiloh's, a dog barks once and then goes quiet. *Probably that Bocephus.*

I turn back to shut the door and as I do, I notice the Louisville slugger just inside, leaning into the corner. Picking it up, I shut the door and take the few steps down into the yard.

After a snowfall there's a hush. It's cotton wool for the world, muting the sharp edges and muffling sound. As I step into that hush, my boots crunch against the thin crust, icy bits finding their way into my shoes to prick at my feet.

I ignore the discomfort, stepping slowly and carefully around the corner of the house.

Footprints. This stretch of snow is trampled with them and I stop, trying to figure them out. They're all over the side yard, crossing each other and trailing in different directions before seeming to turn and trace back. There is no discernible pattern. It's as if the man who made them was pacing, angrily, if the churned-up snow is any indication.

There had been no visible footprints in the front. He had likely stood on the mostly clear driveway or sidewalk, where the snow wasn't sticking.

I move on to the back of the house, following a single line of prints that breaks loose of the others like a string unwinding from a skein of yarn. They are more controlled back here, leading with obvious destination to one window and then another before pivoting and crossing the expanse of back yard.

I follow, bat at the ready. My feeling is that the fucker is long gone, but it would give me great pleasure if he weren't.

From a distance, I hear the sound of sirens. Shiloh must have called. I hurry on into the tree line that separates her property from her neighbor, wanting to find—

Oh, you fucker.

I barely manage to catch myself before I step into a puddle of crimson, the blood almost black against the white snow. Feet away, a dog lies crumpled in a heap, more blood seeping from a wound I can't make out.

Tears sting my eyes and I move closer, making sure not to disturb the ground. "You asshole. You cold fucking motherfucker." All I can do is curse. I have no other words.

Reaching the dog, a hound of some type, I press two fingers to its neck, searching for a pulse. After a few agonizing seconds, I find it, weak, but there.

The dog's alive. I let out my breath in a whoosh and drop my head, pass one hand in a soothing gesture over the animal's fur before I start to gently search for his wound. He lets out a low whine when I find a deep slash in his fur and I place my palm on his head. "It's all right, Bocephus. Hang in there, boy."

I take off my jacket and then my tee shirt, replacing the jacket before I press the shirt to the wound, petting the animal when he whines again.

I need to get back inside with Shiloh. The police are no doubt there by now and she's probably freaking out that I haven't returned, but I can't bring myself to leave the dog. This kind of casual cruelty sickens me.

I hear voices approaching and call out.

"Over here. There's an injured dog. Be careful."

Two officers step gingerly into the area where we sit, partially concealed by the tree line. They hold their guns before them, expressions alert.

"Holy shit," one mutters before looking at me. "You Gunner?"

I nod. "I think this dog belongs to the neighbor." I gesture at the house. "He's alive. He needs help."

"Okay, son. We'll take care of it." He nods to his partner and she takes a few steps away, speaking in low tones on her radio. "No sign of the intruder?"

I shake my head. "I heard the dog bark once when I stepped outside. I think he must have surprised him as he was leaving."

He nods. "Sounds like. Okay, let's get you back inside. We'll take care of the dog. You know his name?"

"I think it's Bocephus."

"If his name's Bocephus, I'm sure he's a tough sonofabitch."

An unwilling smile curves my lips and I stand, giving one last stroke to the dog. "Yeah. There's that. You'll let the neighbor know?"

"Already on it." He inclines his head to his partner, and I see her crossing the back yard to the neighbor's home. "Go on. I'll stay here, but the officers in the house need to get your statement."

I nod and force myself to walk away. Something tells me it's going to be a long ass night.

14
Shiloh

EXHAUSTION TUGS AT ME WHEN GUNNER AND I FINALLY SAY GOODNIGHT TO THE POLICE AND CLOSE THE DOOR BEHIND THEM. I walk into the living room, Gunner's hand a reassuring weight on the nape of my neck as he follows. The lights are off, but the Christmas tree glows and I don't bother turning them on. When the cops were here and busy with me, Gunner cleaned up the glass and nailed a square of plywood he'd found somewhere over the broken panes. As much of an eyesore as it is, at least I know he's not out there, looking in on me.

It's something.

I sink onto the couch and lean back into the cushions, rubbing my eyes with the heels of my hands.

"I can't believe this is still happening," I say, and Gunner sits beside me, tugging me into a loose embrace. "We've got to do something, Gunner. I don't feel like anyone's doing anything. I just go one day to the next, waiting for the next thing to happen."

He squeezes me more tightly to him, and although I'm in no mood to be placated, I melt against his strength. This, I can do. Lean on him. Take the strength he offers. "Hopefully Twiggy will have something for us tomorrow," he replies. "I spoke to her earlier today."

"He hurt an animal. A dog, for heaven's sake. Bocephus wouldn't hurt a fly." Anger fills me at the thought. "If there's nothing on the two she's checking out, I want every man that's ever been around me looked into." A stretch, I know, but I'm past the point of being reasonable. "I'm so tired, Gunner."

"I know, *dolcezza*. Me, too. Lay your head down." I can tell from his tone that he understands I don't just mean physically. We're both mentally, physically, and emotionally drained. I lay my head against his chest.

"We're sleeping here?" His voice is drowsy.

I curl into him, twining my arms around his waist. "I'm not moving," I reply. The room is quiet until a few minutes later, when he whispers into the dim light still coming from the tree. "'Night, love."

THE COLD WAKES ME.

The cold at my back, that is. There's a frigid draft at my backside, likely emanating from the plywood cover across the window. My front, though, is snuggled into Gunner, who at some point stretched out along the sofa and pulled me with him.

My front is toasty warm, and I lie there, face tucked into the dip of his throat, breathing him in. My arms are folded in front of my chest, palms together like I'm praying, and I turn them out, placing them on Gunner's chest.

He's not wearing a shirt—took it off, he said, when I asked about its whereabouts last night, to staunch the dog's blood flow—and his skin is hot to the touch. I can't get any closer to him, and yet my body tries with no direction from my brain to do exactly that, my knee wedging itself in more tightly between his own as I shift forward.

"Mornin'." His voice is rough with sleep and low in tenor, and like always, moves like a caress over my nerve endings. I shiver, and the arm he has draped around my waist makes a languid stroke up my back and then down again, pausing at its original resting place before continuing on to cup and squeeze to my ass.

"Mornin'," I return, and try to play it cool. What happens now? Should I get up? How low long do we just lie here? Is he going to try to kiss me, because I'm sure I'm rocking some stank breath right now.

"I can hear you thinking," he drawls.

"Just deciding on breakfast." I'm a breakfast eater. Always have been, even if it's a donut.

It's possible Gunner really can hear me thinking, because he squeezes my ass again and asks, "how about Karli's?"

I ponder briefly, wondering if returning to Karli's will bring back bad memories. Squaring my shoulders as best I can in my position, I decide that the incident in the parking lot is not going to put me off my sugar fix. Besides, Gunner will be with me.

"Karli's is good." Decision made, I move to stand up, but Gunner hauls me back down against him.

"Wait." He angles just face toward mine. "Kiss."

"Ugh, no. Boys are ick." I wriggle away and he follows.

"Maybe I'll just—" He leans in and swipes his tongue over my cheek.

"You did not just...you licked me!"

He lets me go and crosses his arms behind his head as I scrub at my cheek, face lit with smug satisfaction. "Next time give me a kiss."

"You are gross."

"That must be why you're staring."

I jerk my gaze, which might possibly be fixed on his chest, up to his face. And then I stick my tongue out, because *jerk*.

"Must be," I tease, and flee for the door. Then, because I can and because it feels so good to be...light...after the events of the night, I stick my head back inside. "It's a damn shame you're so ugly."

AFTER RETURNING FROM KARLI'S, we spend the afternoon decorating my Christmas tree. I'm not sure I even want to do it, my holiday spirit on the decline after the rock through my window. But I pull out the box of homemade ornaments and we do so anyway. It feels like giving up if I don't, and I refuse to give up.

Gunner does my least favorite part, fluffing the branches, while I sort the ornaments into piles of glass balls, large ornaments for the bottom of the tree, and fragile ones for the top. We giggle over Sammy's plastic

Star Wars ornament and the ballerina with my name painted across it. We had special ornaments each year, along with the various misshapen salt dough shapes, creating a hodge podge assortment that makes my heart swell with memories.

As Gunner places our ancient angel carefully on the top spike, I step back to take a photo for Sammy with my phone. One photo becomes several, as Gunner's hands holding the delicate angel catch my eye. "Wait." I stop him as he's about to step off the stool and pull a nearby chair over so I can climb up for a better angle. I zoom in on the strength of his hands juxtaposed with the delicate, faded lace of the angel's dress, transfixed by the dichotomy.

There's a knock at the door, and I startle. Gunner reaches out to steady me, his hand at my waist a gentle restraint. "I'll see who it is," he says, stepping down.

I follow behind and see a stranger when Gunner opens the door.

"Hi." He's an older man, thin and wiry in Dickies and a plain jacket. He stands uncertainly for a moment before spotting me behind Gunner and continuing. "Miz Shiloh, you probably don't remember me. You and your brother used to come and play in my garden every year."

The past rushes back. "Mr. Riley!" It's been several years since I've seen him, but I recognize him now. I slide past Gunner and hug him. "Gunner, this is Oscar Riley. He lives in the house behind me. Bocephus—" My voice breaks and I have to stop and clear my throat.

In the pause, Mr. Riley reaches out to shake Gunner's hand. "You must be the young man that found my Bocephus."

Gunner nods. "I'm so sorry about what happened, sir. How is he?"

"He's going to make it, thanks to you. Using your shirt the way you did helped save his life."

"Oh, thank God," I murmur. "Mr. Riley, would you like to come in and have some tea? Coffee?"

"No, no. I just wanted to come by and say thank you. I've had that old boy a long time."

Gunner shuffles his feet and shoves his hands in his pockets in a show of humility. "I did what anyone would do, sir."

Mr. Riley waves a hand in dismissal. "Anyway. You come over and visit me sometime, young lady. You kids have a good holiday."

I wrap an arm around Gunner's waist as we watch him leave. "I'm so glad Bocephus is going to be okay." Gunner shakes his head, a hint of red brightening his cheeks, and we step back inside and close the door behind us.

"I'm going to make some hot chocolate. Want some?" I head toward the kitchen, toeing my clogs off as I go. A cup of something hot and a cuddle on the couch sounds heavenly right now.

Gunner murmurs a distracted affirmative behind me and I glance back to see him peering at his phone, a peculiar expression tightening his features.

"What is it?"

"It's one of the guys that works the vineyard. He was checking on the barrels and says he's not sure, but it looks like someone might have messed with a few of them." He runs a hand behind his head in frustration. "I'm going to have to go check this out since Dad's at the cabin." He makes a face. "He's probably going to have to come home."

"Do you think…?" I'm afraid to finish the thought. It's stupid of me, but I hadn't once considered that my stalker might cross over to Gunner's vineyard.

He leaves the question hanging between us, knowing what I'm asking and choosing not to answer. "I'll be back as soon as I can," he says instead. "But it might be late. Do you have a key in case you're asleep?"

"I have a spare." I pull my purse from the hook beside the door and dig until I find the key. "But you don't need to drive back if it's really late. I have the new locks on all the doors and window. I'll be okay."

He levels a look at me that calls me an idiot for suggesting such a thing. "I'm calling Brodie to come and keep an eye on things while I'm gone," he says, ignoring my statement, and after a single hard press of his lips against mine, is gone.

15
Gunner

IT'S WELL AFTER MIDNIGHT WHEN THE LOW BUZZ of some annoying insect penetrates the fog of sleep I'm deep within. It takes me a minute to figure out that the bug isn't a bug at all, but my cell phone, resting alongside me on the couch. I just sat down for just a minute to rest my eyes. I must have fallen asleep.

I pick the phone up and thumb the notification to allow the Facetime call. "'lo?" My voice is gravel and rust, and I clear my throat, repeating myself as I struggle to focus. Then Shiloh's face fills the screen and I'm fully awake in an instant. "Shiloh? What's wrong?"

"Gunner...I need you...Please—" She's crying and my gut clenches.

"I'm on the way." I'm already up, not hesitating, pushing one foot and then the other into my shoes. "Fucking fell asleep," I mutter, and then I'm scooping my keys off the table and moving out the door in a matter of minutes. "What's going on? Are you hurt? Is someone in the house?"

"What? No. I don't think so." She looks over her shoulder and I realized she's terrified. "He texted me. He's watching me. I thought all the cameras were gone but he must have gotten in and put more in...I need to hide, Gunner. I don't want him watching me." More tears spill down her cheeks and the phone shakes as she swipes at them with her free hand. I've never seen her this way, almost childlike. Ferocity and dignity radiate from Shiloh in every other situation I've seen her in. She was angry and tired last night, upset over the dog, but furious all the same. She raged when that fucker stole her bracelet, held her pride in her middle finger and waved it like a flag when she was all but fired, freaking confronted some random guy in her yard in the middle of the night—but this! Whatever this is; it has her near collapse and my hand shakes as I jam the keys in the ignition and twist.

Fury rises in me at the recognition, and I want to lay hands on the one responsible.

"Okay. I'll be there in just a few minutes, *dolcezza*. How about the bathroom? Can you lock yourself in there?" Where the fuck is Brodie? Doesn't he realize something is happening inside the house?

"No! Not the bathroom."

"Okay, okay, not there. Pantry again?" Traffic is light and I'm able to make my way to her house virtually unmolested, the intermittent stoplights along the way staying green, as if they know I wouldn't pay them any heed anyway.

"Pantry…okay…" She breathes heavily as she makes her way to the pantry, and then I hear the creak of a door as it opens and shuts.

"Locked in?"

"Yes." She's marginally calmer.

"Good girl. I'm almost there." Silence hangs heavy on the line for a minute. In my periphery I can see her face, scared and not looking anywhere other than the screen. "Shiloh, do you think there's somebody there? In the house, I mean?"

She shakes her head, the smallest of movements, but I catch it.

Silence.

"Talk to me, Shiloh."

"You talk," she snaps. "I can't think right now." *There's my girl.*

"Okay. I'll talk." I rack my brain for something light. "This wasn't how I pictured you waking me up in the middle of the night, Shy." I hear her breath catch. "Are you going to ask me what I pictured?"

I can't look at her while I'm driving to see her reaction, but I know she can see me, the occasional streetlight flashing over my face. Her hesitation is a palpable thing before her whisper comes, soft and near tangible in the dark of the car. It murmurs across my skin, raising gooseflesh. "Tell me."

"We're in bed, sound asleep because we wore each other out earlier. But a dream wakes you, and you're soaking wet and so needy. I feel your fingers, first on my collarbone. Then you walk them down the center of my abs, and then circle them slowly around my cock. I'm rock hard for you immediately, no questions asked. Just like always." There is a slow inhale, a measured exhale. "And then your fingers are followed by your warm, wet mouth –"

"Enough." Her voice is strangled, and I smile at the obvious effect I have on her. I'm glad it's not one-sided, glad I can make her suffer a tenth of what she does me.

And then I'm pulling in the driveway. From the shadows, Brodie detaches himself and walks quickly toward me. Relief floods me that he came when I called him earlier in the evening, that he's been here to keep watch. *So much for time off,* he snarked a bit, but he came.

"Everything all right?" He looks at the darkened house with concern as I step out of the truck.

"Shiloh's on the line. Sounds like the fucker got in and planted some cameras and such to replace the ones we pulled. He's messing with her."

"Ah, balls. You're staying?"

"Taking her with me. You can head out."

"Right. Thanks, man."

"I'm here, now, Shiloh. Coming to the door." I disconnect, and a moment later she answers my knock, shivering in what I've come to realize is her customary tee and sleep shorts. Without waiting for permission, I pull her into me tightly, trying to quell her shaking. I smooth my hands up and down her back, trying to calm her as best I know how before I pick her up altogether. She clings to me like a monkey, legs going around my waist to cross behind me at the ankles. I hold her like this for several long minutes, until I feel her trembles subsiding.

I carry her to the bedroom and set her down on the bed before I begin pulling clothes out of drawers and tossing them on the bed. There's a pair of sweats on the end and I toss those to her, watching as she pulls them on, covering her legs an inch at a time. "Get what you need. We're leaving."

For the barest second, I think she's going to argue. Then she gives a clipped nod and pulls a duffel from beneath the bed. "Use this." She retreats to the bathroom and returns with an arm load of girly shit, dumping it in the bag. Then she pulls a utilitarian looking leather bag from the closet and tucks her laptop into a compartment.

I catch a glimpse of a heavy-duty looking camera as I grab the duffel and start stuffing.

She side-eyes me as I grab numerous panties and bras from the top drawer, tossing a few pair of jeans and tees on top. "Actual clothes, too, please."

"Fun killer," I complain. "Ready?"

She takes a look around. "Yeah. That's good for now." We leave and make the return drive in silence. Wrapping my fingers of my left hand around the steering wheel, I place the other on her leg, letting my fingers wrap around her thigh and squeeze lightly. A promise of future intimacy.

Back at my home, I lead her to the pool house and hold out my hand. "Let me see the text." Shiloh purses her lips.

"I'm here now. It's done. I'd rather you didn't."

"Shiloh."

Her cheeks are bright red. "It's embarrassing. Disgusting."

"Just give me the damn phone."

Her eyes fill with tears and she slaps it in my hand after unlocking it. I find the text and realize immediately why Shiloh didn't want me to see it. "That fucker videoed you in the bath." I say the words calmly, but inside I'm committing all sorts of mayhem. I'm bathing in blood, breaking necks, and crunching the bones of psycho perverts who think this sort of thing is okay.

The video is accompanied by a string of messages.

I see you're thinking of me.

I'm thinking of you, too.

I watch this and imagine I'm there with you.

It won't be long now.

The things I'll do to you.

But first you'll be punished.

You're going to love it.

They go on and on, increasingly profane. It's no wonder Shiloh was in the state she was by the time I made it to her, frightened of shadows. Using my phone, I shoot off a quick text to Twiggy that I need some tech help on the phone.

Either Twiggy and the police missed a camera, or he went back and installed more. His escalation is starting to make sense. He's watching us together, watching Shiloh closely. He must have seen something—maybe Shiloh and me in her house at some point—and become angry. And later got off to a video of her in the bath having what is very clearly a private moment.

White hot anger flashes through me at the thought of anyone other than me seeing her like that. Her head tipped back, eyes closed, and lips parted. Breasts jutting sleek and wet just above the water while her hand worked under its surface. *Mine.*

I hear a crack and looked down to see I've cracked her phone screen. "Shit. I'm sorry, Shiloh."

Shiloh wraps her arms around herself. "It's okay. I was going to get another one, anyway. With a different number."

I nod. "We can take care of it tomorrow." I tip her chin up, forcing her to make eye contact with me "Shy. Look at me. This is not disgusting. What's disgusting is this pervert. I'm going to take care of this asshole, okay? I don't want you to worry about him or be scared. Got it? You can trust me. Today, tomorrow, a year from now."

She looks at me for a long minute, hazel eyes troubled, before nodding. "Got it." She gives me a small smile that fails to reach her eyes. "I trust you, Gunner."

I kiss her, quick, reassuring, and deliberately devoid of passion. That's not what she needs right now. "Good, now go to bed. We'll talk more about this in the morning." At her panicked look, I gesture to the chaise at the foot of the bed. "I'll be right here if you need me. Not going anywhere."

"That's too short for you, Gunner; you'll hang off the end."

"I'll be fine."

"But—"

"Shiloh." I back her into the bed, pushing her into the mattress gently. "I really need you to lay down right now, under a big pile of blankets, so I can't see or touch this freckle here…" I dip my head and touch my tongue to the freckle just above her belly button. "…or this one here." I find another one on the crest of her shoulder by pushing her tee shirt aside and rub it gently with my scruff, smiling when I feel her shudder. "It may make me a bastard, but if you don't, I won't be able to keep my hands off you after seeing that video. And that's not a memory I want in your head. Okay?"

Her face falls. "No…not okay."

"I'm sorry. I shouldn't have…fuck, I'm a jackass." I rake my hand through my hair.

"No—that's not what I mean." Her hands twist together at her waist and she's looking everywhere but my face.

"What are you saying, Shiloh?"

"I'm saying I need you to hold me, Gunner. Can you just hold me?"

"Oh." Relief that I didn't add to the problem makes me smile. "Yeah, *dolcezza*. I can do that." I turn off the lights and undress down to my boxer briefs, then study the space she's left for me in the king-sized bed. She's in the middle, on her side. Climbing in beside her, I will my dick into submission and gather her close to me, little spoon to my big spoon. She sighs, relaxing as she exhales, and a surge of protectiveness floods through me. Kissing the top of her head, I squeeze her just a little closer.

Mine.

16
Shiloh

I WAKE SLOWLY, my thoughts muddied but my body instantly aware of the situation it's in. I should have thought about this last night when I was begging Gunner to *hold me, please, Gunner, I just need to be held*...I roll my eyes at my own ignorance and try to figure out how to extricate myself. A quickie before Gunner goes to school isn't really on my list of perfect ways to lose my virginity.

But, oh. The feels. The sensations of his heavy arm in residence between my breasts, his warm breath fanning my neck, and his morning wood poking my ass make me want to stretch and purr and rub up against him like a cat in heat.

As if my thoughts communicate themselves telepathically to him, somehow, Gunner shifts and thrusts his hips lazily into my backside. His hand, the one between my breasts, flattens and splays out between them, pulling me back into him more securely and raising my alarm levels to def con-five. I elbow him and hiss. "Gunner!"

In response he arches his hips into me once again and moves a hand to sleepily cover and squeeze my boob. I try again. "Gunner! Wake up!"

I'm twisting my torso to try to wrangle myself out from under him when his eyes open. They flare and then hood with immediate desire, shielding that intense silvery gray. I put my hand over my mouth to cover my morning breath. "Umm...morning?"

His lips quirk and he squeezes my boob, before moving a thumb in a leisurely circle over my nipple. "Same." He watches me with lazy intent. "Move your hand."

"I have morning breath–" My words come out muffled behind my hand.

"We'll have it together." Brushing my hand away, he dips his head down to lick into my mouth, and as my belly tightens with desire, the last thing I'm thinking about is toothpaste. Gunner shifts and raises himself above me, trailing open-mouthed kisses along my jaw and neck as one hand goes to the hem of the tee shirt I slept in. He pauses and looks at me, wordlessly asking permission, and I grant it with a faint nod. With a quick motion, he divests me of the shirt, and I'm bared before him. It's nothing he hasn't seen, but he still gazes upon my breasts with something like wonder, holding himself up on one arm while he uses the free hand to touch lightly, almost reverently. My nipples peak to painful points under his light exploration, and I grit my teeth.

"Touch me, damnit."

He levels me with a look. "As you wish, *dolcezza*."

"No room for a Wesley…in this relationship…aah…God…" His mouth is on my breast, sucking deep and firm and shutting me up with efficacy. He circles the peak with his tongue as he sucks, one hand under my back to provide support as I arch, helpless against his clever mouth. He uses his other hand on my waiting breast, switching his attentions only when I am a writhing, helpless mess before him.

As I lay back against the bed, panting and near delirium, he pauses and sits back. I start to sit up, thinking to do something for him, but he places his large hand in the center of my chest and gently presses me back down on his dark navy sheets. "Lay down and let me look."

"Oh." I fight the urge to cover my breasts as his gaze lingers on me. It inspires more nervousness, strangely, than a room full of faceless men, whistling and tossing money on the stage. Instead of covering myself, though, I submerge my shaky trust issues and instead raise my arms over my head. I'm rewarded with the audible quickening of his breath. He reaches a finger out, tracing first one peak, then another before sliding both hands down to just below my waist.

"Your tits...Shiloh, you don't even know how amazing your tits are."

His thumb dips into my navel and then with no further ceremony he's pulling my underwear over my hips and off.

Hunger glints in his eyes, turning them to liquid steel as he looks at me. I squirm; feeling pinned under his gaze like a butterfly on a board and squeeze my legs together to stem the sudden rush of sensation.

"Don't," he says, and places the palm of his hand heavy and warm against the neatly trimmed hair of my pussy, fingers arrowed toward my toes. "Mine. Every time I look at you, that's what I think. That even if you don't know it yet, you're mine. This body..." He raises his eyes to mine and applies a gentle seeking pressure at that most sensitive part of me. "This heart." When I give him a shaky nod, he pushes my thighs wide, dips his head, and inspires the fleeing of rational thought with the carnal touch of his mouth on my seam.

His tongue moves against me with surety: hot, wet, demanding, and more than anything I've ever felt before.

He uses one arm just under my bottom to prop me up and open, and spreads the other across my lower belly, pinning me in place when I would twist away at the sheer torment of his mouth. Dimly, I wonder how the hell he knows how to do this with this level of expertise, but all I can do is twist my hands in his hair and hold on.

Against my folds, I feel, rather than hear, him chuckle. He's gentle but demanding, each tug on that most sensitive part of me commanding complete obeisance to his ruthlessness. "Talk to me, Shiloh," he says, and I gasp.

"Whaa?"

"Tell me what you like." He swirls his tongue and I moan. "That's it."

"That. I like that."

"Use your words, *dolcezza*." He sucks hard, and I see stars. A ragged groan escapes me.

"Words…" Gunner chuckles again, and then does something with his tongue that has me shaking, flattening it against me. He slips a finger in me at the same time, pushing against my clit from the opposite direction. "Oh, God, oh, God, oh God…"

"Just me, my tongue, and your pussy, *dolcezza*."

"I love your tongue, Gunner."

"My tongue loves your pussy, Shy."

"Gunner. Please stop talking." I press upward against his face, begging wordlessly for what I want.

"With pleasure." Gunner doesn't leave me unsatisfied. He devours me. I've never done this before with anyone, always thinking it sounded like something a guy wouldn't be into. Gunner is eating me, though, like I'm his favorite soft serve ice cream on a hot day, melting all over the cone. I'm almost embarrassed by the wetness seeping out of me, the sounds my body makes as he licks me, but if anything, it seems to spur him on. He increases the pressure, tugging me more firmly into the dark heat of his mouth.

My thighs tremble and press more firmly against his head. He grips them in his hands and spreads me wide, looking down at my wetness for a moment.

Then he sucks my clit between his teeth and gently bites.

It ends me. I shudder and fight his hands holding me open, needing to clench my thighs hard around his head, my body bowing up off the bed as I pulse in breathless paroxysms against his face. I'm left boneless and gasping, my heart beating too fast in my chest, as he nuzzles his face against my hip tenderly and then sits.

"God, you're sweet." He studies me without speaking as I lay sprawled limply out before him, then leans over to kiss me, brief and sweet. He rises and I sit, realizing that we're done for the moment.

"Wait! What about…aren't we going to?" I suddenly feel like a twelve-year-old.

"That was all for you, pretty girl. I'm good. I'm going to grab a shower and some breakfast, make sure Nonna knows you're here, and then I have to run to school. I need to get your phone to Twiggy after so she can try to trace the texts, so I may be a few minutes late getting back. You'll be okay?"

"Yes, of course." I can't help feeling a little depressed, even though I understand that he has to go. Of course he wasn't going to be able to hang out and cuddle. And then his words hit me.

"Nonna's here? Your family?"

"They got back late last night."

"We need to talk about what happened here."

"Later. Someone made me late." He grins to take the sting out of the words. "Go over and eat with Nonna when you're ready, okay?" I put on a smile and nod, and he tucks a hand around the back of my neck, pulling me in for another kiss that makes my toes curl. He punctuates it with a whisper that goes straight to my core and makes it bloom with heat.

"You taste..." Another quick kiss. "...so fucking..." Kiss. "...sweet." One final kiss, and then he's gone, crossing the room to the adjoined bathroom.

17
Gunner

SHILOH'S TASTE LINGERS IN MY MEMORY as I walk across the lawn between the pool house and the main house, not banished by brushing my teeth and taking a shower. God, she was so fucking sweet. Leaving her lying there in my bed, all snugged up under my comforter, reddish hair fanning out over my pillow was one of the hardest things I've had to do in recent days.

I wanted to crawl back into bed with her. Run my fingers through that hair and hold the strands up to let it catch the light, filter the sun like the bottle of Hennessy whiskey sitting in dad's study. Bury my face in that valley between her breasts and let myself suffocate in her scent, that heady blend of vanilla, lavender, and citrus.

I understand what the good book meant, now, when it talked about lying with someone. I want to lie with Shiloh, and never rise.

But I have to go to fucking school, and make sure that I get her phone to Twiggy later so she can work on tracing the text messages. It probably won't accomplish much, but I'll keep trying. Maybe he would get sloppy sooner or later.

I send her a text. Might as well let her know I'll be by later.

I'm surprised when she calls as I reach the back terrace. I take the call outside, not wanting Nonna's keen ears hearing everything.

"What's up?"

"Just got your message, so that's fine. I'll be here. I have some preliminary results, too, on those guys you asked me about. Now a good time?"

"Yeah, sure. Hit me with it."

"Okay, first. Dr. Jason Adams, thirty-seven years old, adopted by Samuel and Beatrice Thurston. Younger adopted brother, Theo. Exemplary academic record taking him through college and med school. The brother was a complete hell-raiser, though, was cut-off by the mother. Nothing that raises any flags, except maybe that he's unmarried."

I grunt. "Okay. Next?"

"Next is Daniel Mathis, forty-two years old. He's a transplant from the New York city area, and has been working at the club for the past twelve years. Not a lot to him. He's not married, either, and is a little sleazy—has a total thing for young women—but I'm not sure he has the brain power to stalk someone without getting caught. He was a loser in high school. Drugs, petty theft that he managed to keep pretty well hidden on his application to Kendricks. The one thing I don't like about Mathis is that he did have a note on his record about a dismissed charge—cops found an underage girl in his apartment after a concert in Charlottesville several years ago."

"He sounds pretty good for it, don't you think?"

"I don't know. Almost too good, you know? Like I said, I just don't think he's that smart. I think he's just a creep."

"All right, I'll keep an open mind. What about Reasor?"

"I think he's okay, but here's what I found. Twenty-three years old, assistant football coach…you know all that. He's been open about his obsession with Shiloh. It was only made worse when she briefly dated and then dumped him their senior year."

"He cheated on her."

"Yeah, I know. Anyway, I think it was a hit to his big man on campus rep. I didn't find too much about his home life. Mother, father, stable home. Father died a few years back of liver complications. I think there may have been some abuse when he was a child. I managed to find an old CPS report. Teacher called after he made some comment in class. Nothing ever came of it, though."

"Wow. This is good stuff, Twig."

"Mostly preliminary. That's the first layer. I'm digging down."

"All right, well, maybe you'll have more this afternoon."

"Maybe. See you later, then."

I disconnect, mind buzzing with the information Twig has thrown my way. Opening the back door, I walk in the kitchen to see Nonna busy at the stove. They got in late last night, but I'm sure she was up with the sunrise as usual. She tilts her cheek up for me to greet her with my customary kiss, and I steal a breakfast cookie as I do so from the platter beside her. The thick, crumbly cookies are a staple in our household, perfect for dipping in creamy coffee or, when I was younger, hot chocolate.

"Good morning, Nonna."

"Morning, *polpetto*. Did you sleep well?"

It's a common enough question between us, one I don't normally pause and think twice about answering. There's a gleam in her eye, though, that warns me to tread carefully. "Well enough," I answer.

"And how about that pretty girl in the pool house, hmmm?"

I knew it. Nothing is sacred in this house. The old woman knows everything, somehow. Wondering how on earth she already knows about Shiloh's presence, I take my time answering, fixing myself a heaping plate of bacon, eggs, and biscuits, a glass of juice, and a cup of coffee before I take my place at the bar. All the while, Nonna watches me in narrow-eyed silence.

"How'd you know about her?" I finally mumble through a mouthful of eggs. Nonna smacks my hand.

"Manners, *polpetto*! Were you raised in a barn?"

"Yes, ma'am. No, ma'am." Sheepish, I finish chewing.

"Don't worry about how I know. Your *nonna* knows things. Nonna knows everything." She sits across from me at the bar, her iron and white hair neatly twisted in a bun on top of her head. She wears, as she has for all the years I've known her, a simple cotton housedress and an apron over top paired with comfortable orthopedic shoes. I eye her over the top of the coffee I'm sipping and shake my head.

"You are one scary lady, old woman." She waits me out, well aware of this little game we play, where I pretend like I'm not going to talk, and she pretends like she's giving me a choice. It's pretty much the reason I told Shiloh to come over and get breakfast. If I hadn't, I knew Nonna would be in the pool house within five minutes of my leaving.

"It's not a big deal, Nonna," I finally say. "Her name's Shiloh Brookings. She's Sammy's older sister, I'm kind of crazy about her, and don't tell anyone, but I'm pretty sure I'm going to marry that girl someday."

"Oh…well, if that's all." She tries for nonchalance, but her eyes twinkle. "I remember Sammy Brookings. So this Shiloh…she's a bit older than you?"

"Yes, almost three years."

"That's not too much."

"No, it's good." I point my fork at her sternly. "And I mean it, Nonna. Absolutely, under no circumstances, do you meddle. Do not go saying anything to Shiloh. She's skittish."

"Ah, *polpetto*. You haven't…how you say…put a ring on it?" I laugh, loudly.

"I think that song is talking about a wedding ring. You'll know when I get to that part."

She looks nonplussed. "But why is she skittish? You are a good boy! Handsome boy! Good family! What's wrong with her?"

I wonder how best to explain without betraying Shiloh's confidence. "She has a complicated history, Nonna. It's difficult for her to trust people. But I'm making progress."

"Hmmm." Her gaze is turned inward as she thinks for a while. "Are you being romantic, *polpetto*? And I don't mean sexy. I mean romantic."

I'm a little twitchy at the idea of discussing romance with my *nonna*, but I rub the back of my neck and plow ahead. "You mean flowers and shit?"

"Language, young man!"

"I'm sorry, Nonna."

"You are forgiven. But yes, flowers. And stuff."

"Nonna, flowers are dumb. They're dead in a few days. I could get her…I don't know…a new memory card for her camera or something?"

Nonna rolls her eyes. "You miss the point, *polpetto*. It doesn't matter that the flowers will die. That you gave them to her says you saw them and thought about her. If you had to pick a flower, which one would remind you of your Shiloh?"

I think. Shiloh is unrestrained, bold, fierce. She's also bound by her past, responsibilities, perceived conventions. She's a conundrum. A contradiction. Soft on the inside, prickly on the outside. A rose would work, but it's too cliché.

"A cactus?" I suggest. Nonna's brow wrinkles.

"Hmmm. Well...you'll have to think about that one a bit more, I think. But think about romance this way. Say she wants to go on a picnic. You go, and you eat, and you talk, and you drink wine. Maybe you share a kiss. You share the same experience, but it's very different for each of you. Your girl, she went on this picnic for the conversation, and her man's company, and the bottle of wine...the romance of it. You went on the picnic to eat the food, no? And the whole time you're wondering why on earth your girl chose to do this thing in the park, sitting on the ground on a blanket where ants can crawl all over the food." I snort. "This is the difference, *polpetto*, between a practical man and a romantic woman. Your girl can buy her own memory card. But she won't buy herself flowers."

"I get it. But how is that going to help her trust me?"

Nonna shakes her head. "If she trusts you with her heart, she'll trust you with other things. And vice versa."

Strangely, it makes sense. "Thanks, Nonna. Listen, I have to go. I told Shiloh to come over and eat when she gets up, so you should meet her in a bit. Also..."

"Yes?"

"Why don't you put together a picnic dinner for me and Shiloh for this evening? With a classy bottle of our finest?"

"A picnic, *polpetto*? There's snow on the ground!"

"Hey. Don't knock it 'til you try it."

Nonna snaps a dishtowel at me. "Good luck with that."

18
Shiloh

GUNNER'S *NONNA* IS SOMETHING ELSE. A petite woman with steel wool hair pulled neatly up into a bun, she sits across from me as I eat the most scrumptious breakfast cookies I've ever tasted, studying me openly. I feel a little like a circus freak on display, but there's nothing offensive in her perusal of me. It's curiosity—frank, honest, simple. She's wondering how Gunner and I came to be together. How I came to be in the pool house last night. What kind of issues I have.

If I'm going to hurt Gunner.

"This is delicious," I murmur, hoping to ease the tension. "My thighs thank you."

"Is Italian," she replies. "And your thighs need the help. Too skinny. Is best to dunk." She shows me, dunking her own cookie in her milky coffee. I mimic her actions and close my eyes in bliss at the flavors. The slight bitterness of the coffee, coupled with the sweetness of the pastry is divine, tugging a moan from me. "Is good, no?"

"Oh...so good." A thought strikes me. "I love to bake. It's kind of a hobby of mine. Would you teach me how to make these sometime?"

Her eyes light up, and she slips from the stool. Before I can another word, she's tossing me an apron and pulling a mixing bowl from a cabinet. "Esme, she has no interest in the kitchen," she grouses as she marches to what I presume is a pantry, coming back moments later with her arms full of ingredients. "I will teach you, *dolcezza*. Right here, please."

As she mixes and measures, showing me her careful notes passed down from her mother, I find Nonna's no-nonsense demeanor stealthily slipping into the hole left by my mother when she died. It is a balm to my spirit that conversely leaves me edgy and restless. My fingers itch for my camera. I want to capture Nonna's hands in the dough, crumbly bits clinging to her papery skin. Maybe a shot from above of that iron hair bent over her task. It reminds me of all of the photos of my mother I'll never be able to capture, all the ones I never thought about when she was here.

As soon as I can politely do so when the cookies are finished, I excuse myself.

"Oh, Shiloh—"

I turn back at the door. "Yes?"

"Gunner left that envelope for you."

"Thank you, Nonna." I pick up the envelope she points to from its resting place on the granite countertop and leave, walking across the yard to the pool house.

I feel so weird being here without Gunner. A fraction the size of the main house, the pool house still echoes around me, spacious and airy with wide-planked floors and a wood-raftered ceiling. Local art hangs on the walls, oil paintings of the mountains and vineyards and places that I assume are in Italy. I wander from one to the next to look at them as I tear the flap on the note Gunner left for me.

Picnic dinner tonight? Be ready to leave when I get back. Bring your camera…you'll want to play.

Curling my fist against my belly, I try to curb the smile that spreads over my face. This boy...he's working my feels department. If I'm not careful, I'm going to catch feelings that I won't be able to let go of when it comes time to say good-bye.

Because as hard as I try, I just can't imagine this lasting.

But for today...

Biting my lip, I pick up the spare phone Gunner left for me and tap a message to his programmed number.

As long as you keep me warm.

GUNNER LOOKS ACROSS AT ME WITH MISCHIEF IN HIS EYES as we bump along a gravel road on vineyard property. It's hard to keep my eyes off him, dressed as he is in a pair of jeans that cling to his thighs and a warm-looking navy pullover that accents the icy quality of his eyes. It hugs his body just the right amount, accentuating the lines of his arms and breadth of his shoulders and revealing how the solid bulk of his chest tapers into a lean waistline.

"See something you like?" He teases, reaching over to flick my ponytail.

I direct my attention ahead. "Not in the least. You're hideous."

He laughs. "You must like ugly." He picks up my hand and brings it to his mouth, pressing a kiss to the center of my palm. I smile.

"Ugh. I just threw up in my mouth a little."

"Bet you're wet."

I slant him a look. "At least the scenery is pretty."

The gravel road is bordered on either side by an ancient-looking split rail fence. Sunlight dapples the road through thick trees, now devoid of greenery. Classic vinyl plays low on the radio as we bump along the gravel for a mile or so, until the trees thin and open to a view that takes my breath away. We're perched at the top of a small valley, looking down upon a vista of sprawling fields of row upon row of pruned grapevines, all dipping down to a small, jewel-like lake nestled at the bottom of the valley's vee.

Most of the snow has already melted off in the day's warmer temps and sunshine, a few spots in shady areas clinging here and there.

Gunner stops the truck at the sound of my breath releasing in a low sigh. "Prettiest spot on the vineyard," he says.

"It's stunning."

The lake is a sterling color at the moment, ripples glinting in the afternoon sun, but I can imagine it in the height of fall, reflecting autumn-hued trees instead of the current early winter dullness. It doesn't bother me, though, the dormancy soothing, even anticipatory. Everything is just waiting to wake up, to feel the faint brush of spring months ahead of us.

My fingers twitch on the windowsill. "Do you mind—"

"If you take pictures?" Gunner smiles. "No. That's why I told you to bring your camera. Just be careful. Ground's going to be soggy and you're still unsteady on that ankle."

I'm climbing out of the truck, camera in hand, before he's finished speaking. "You might as well get comfortable," I tell him. "We might be here a while."

He follows me out of the truck, coming around to me and walking me up against it, caging me against its hood with his forearms on either side of my shoulders. Between us, a hard buffer, the camera hangs from my neck. He leans in close, head dipping down so he can trail his nose along my neck and under my ear. I shiver at the sensation, biting my lip as I allow my head to fall back with a thunk against the truck, and place my hands on his abs. I feel him shudder in response as I scrape lightly with my fingernails, moving the fabric of his shirt against his skin.

"Way ahead of you...I'm going to pull the truck down there..." He kisses my neck and then my jawline. "...between those two rows of vines..." His lips keep moving, the only point of contact between our bodies except for my hands on his stomach.

Focus, Shiloh. There're only a thousand vines down there. I look over his shoulder, trying to figure out where he's referring to. "...while you do your thing. I might even take a nap." He finishes with a light slap on my butt and starts walking back around to the driver's side of the truck while I stare, off-balance. How does he just switch gears like that? He can't be as unaffected as he pretends to be. I lean on the window and look inside and at his lap pointedly, where his erection strains against his jeans, begging to be released.

I smirk. "Okay. Enjoy your nap."

With a wink and a tug on the brim of the hat he pulls on, Gunner drives away. I spend the next hour moving slowly, first along the upper edges of the fields of vine, and then working my way gradually inward. My eye is trained on everything all at once and nothing in particular. I can see a thousand tiny details in the intricate tracery of shadow cast on the ground by a grapevine, but couldn't have said if an army had been hidden behind it. When I start shooting, I become oblivious in moments.

Finally, as the sun is starting to think about dipping behind the mountains, casting them in a purple ombre capped with gold and orange, I make my way to where I can see Gunner's truck. My ankle is aching in its boot and I'm starting to get hungry for that picnic he promised me. A knot settles in my throat when I draw close, though, and I forget my hunger.

Gunner is sacked out in the truck bed, his ball cap tugged down over his eyes and his hands folded over his stomach, where his pullover has drawn up and a strip of skin just shows. He's lain a couple of sleeping bags in the bed, a quilt over top of them, and placed pillows all around the perimeter. It looks cozy and inviting, and he is completely relaxed in the nest he has created, breaths coming even and deep. I raise my camera to take a photo when his voice pauses me with its slow, husky drawl.

"You going to stand there looking, or climb up here with me where you belong?"

I snap the picture swiftly and tuck my camera back in my bag. "Oh, I'm coming." I watch him crane his neck up to look at me as I heft myself onto the tailgate and crawl toward him on the blankets. He lifts his right arm as I come up alongside him, pulling me flush against his body, and I relax into him.

I burrow my head into that delicious spot where his pecs meet his shoulder and inhale the scent of sandalwood and man. It feels natural to bring my arm around his waist, even more so for him to pull that arm even more snugly around him with his own, still resting across his stomach. He grasps my elbow and holds me to him firmly, the minimal contact somehow providing me a level of security that makes me feel safe and treasured.

I close my eyes, allowing myself to drift.

Minutes later, Gunner shifts. I feel his hands glide down my sides as he resettles himself on top of me, careful to keep most of his weight off. I look down at him curiously as he looks up, his face poised just above my belly, expression intent.

"Nonna told me I needed to be romantic with you," he says, fingers creeping under the edge of my sweater. It's chilly out here, and my skin prickles with gooseflesh as he bares it, inch by inch, but I don't feel cold.

His eyes are fire, warming me.

"Romantic, huh?"

"Mm-hmm." He lowers his face to nuzzle my belly, trailing his nose from the waistline of my jeans to my navel and then up to the slight indentation below my rib cage. I remind myself to breathe.

"I don't know...I think you're pretty romantic, Gunner. I've never had another guy bring me donuts or give me poetry before."

"Shiloh."

"Gunner?"

"You ever make love in the back of a pick-up truck?"

My breath hitches. He knows I haven't done that anywhere before, let alone a pickup truck. He's really asking something very different.

He's asking if I trust him.

19
Gunner

HER ANSWER IS A KISS.

She pulls my face up to hers and sighs into my mouth, and if she feels my arms shaking with the need to crush her to me, she doesn't comment. She merely climbs to her knees before me and slowly begins to remove her sweater, her eyes never leaving mine. My eyes flare as I watch her in silence, and then I rise beside her, gently moving her hands. "Let me."

I tug her sweater over her head and unclip her bra, and then my hands rise to cup her shoulders, fingers accompanying her bra straps on their descent and leaving goose bumps in their wake. My lips twist at the sight, and I pull the bra completely off with a single digit, tossing it to join the other clothing in the truck bed. I exalt—no other word for it—in the pebbled flesh the moonlight reveals. I could look at her all night, stare like some callow boy who's never seen a pair of pretty tits before. She's cold, though, the brisk air raising her nipples to stiff points. I want to tongue each one to still more painful hardness, mimicking the hardness of my cock.

"You're sure?" I take a nipple between my thumb and forefinger and squeeze. It peaks further in my grasp and I can't prevent the resultant low growl from escaping. "We can go somewhere else?"

Placing her hand over my heart, she leans down and kisses me softly on the lips. "I'm sure. Finally, I'm sure. No take backs, Gunner." I can tell she's trying to keep it steady, but her voice wavers. "You're the one with the pretty words, so you'll just have to believe me when I say that I've never been more certain. Maybe you knew way back when Krystal Jenkins dared me to give you seven minutes in heaven, but I think a part of me always suspected you'd give me a lifetime. So, I'm ready— *oompf.*"

I don't have pretty words for Shiloh. Not like this. Not a single poem I've come across, no song lyrics stuck in my head. I can only tell her I love her, love every freckle on her body, want to map each and every one like constellations in the sky. I want to know her so profoundly the knowledge of who she is seeps its way into my cells and locks itself away, a permanent part of my DNA. It's always been her. I've waited for her for years, and I'll wait forever longer, if I have to. So I don't answer with words.

Instead, I slice her words into a gasp as I pull her up and into my lap. I grip her butt in my hands and crash my mouth to hers, swallowing anything else she might have said. Her hands are at my waist, tugging my pullover up and over my head and tossing it to the side, her eyes devouring the skin of my chest as hungrily as I did hers. She reaches out to touch me, and her fingertips sear me in the cold air, hot and silky against my skin. And then her hand is headed south, pausing at the placket of my jeans as she raises her eyes to me uncertainly.

Shiloh

LOOKING AT GUNNER, I slide my hands down the dip and swell of his arms, then around to his abdominals. Moving my fingers southward, I pause at the placket of his jeans, beset suddenly with nervousness. His eyes smile at me, a challenge in their depths, and gathering myself, I work at the button. Gunner sucks in a sharp breath, trying to give me some room, and I can feel him, hard and velvety just beneath the waistband. "Let me," he mutters, taking over. "Boots first."

He shifts us so he can tug off his heavy work boots, and I hastily do the same with my one tennis shoe and my boot, and then we're both unbuttoning, unzipping, and easing our jeans down and over our hips until we're left clad in only our only underwear. Gunner shucks his off, too, his eyes intent upon me, but in one last bastion of shyness, I leave mine on.

Not that I have a lot of experience with penises, but Gunner is big. He's a big guy—solid, tall, packed with muscle—and his cock is no different. I swallow, uncertain all of a sudden. He sees me looking at him and his hand takes hold of his cock and pumps it slowly once, twice. Hesitant, I reach out a hand to touch him and he wraps my fingers around him, showing me with a brief squeeze and a hiss of breath the pressure he likes.

Silk over steel. The contrast is fascinating, and I run my palm with a mix of shyness and boldness up, then down.

He reaches for his jeans and pulls a foil packet from his pocket, tearing it open with his teeth. He shows me how to roll it down his length. I wish the layer of latex weren't there, keeping his skin from mine.

His own hand reaches out, tracing the band of lace that edges my panties. First along my pelvis, then my hip bones. I inhale and release him as he tucks his thumbs in the waistband and eases them down, over my hips and legs and feet and then pitches them aside.

Sweeping his hands back up, he cages my rib cage with both hands, measuring its circumference, before moving upward to palm both breasts with reverence, bringing them to his mouth. He pulls first one, then the next, into his mouth, tugging strongly when I dig my nails into the skin on his shoulders and release a shuddering breath. He holds me in place when I squirm away from the pleasure-pain he offers, a large hand square on my back, and I lay my head back and open my eyes to see stars. Stars from the sky, stars from his ministrations...I have no center, no way of knowing.

"*Dolcezza...*" He studies my body as though it were something priceless, pausing here and there to place a kiss at the juncture of my knee, the vee of my legs, my navel. "You make me weak."

Oh, his pretty words.

He drinks from me deeply, as he did this morning, until I am a writhing mess of need in the bed of that truck, begging him for release. After what seems like a thousand years, he's poised above me, tendons of strain cording his neck, his face taut with concentration. He's holding himself up on his elbows, his hands cupping my face as his fingers tenderly move the sweaty strands of my hair back. His cock nudges my entrance, blunt and hard, and I shift my legs further apart to give him room.

"I can't...I don't think I can do slow and sweet, *dolcezza*," he says.

I spare a thought for my virginity and hastily shove it aside. "I'm not afraid." I draw my knees up as Gunner positions himself between my thighs, rubs his cock once, twice against my clit, sending a sharp, aching spear of pleasure racing through me. "I'm good. Fuck me, Gunner."

"One thing straight. This isn't me fucking you, Shy." Despite his earlier statement, he eases into me with excruciating restraint, stilling when I tense. The universe narrows to that single point of sensation, the feel of his thickness filling me, stretching me. Changing me.

My muscles melt around him, relaxing, welcoming him, and I move my hips in a slight, exploratory movement. Gunner hisses. "No. This is me loving you. Knowing you. Owning you. Only *you*. Always *you*. Ever *you*—" Eyes focused on mine, he strokes forward and into me forcefully in tandem with his words, burying himself to the hilt and stopping for a moment, changing in an instant from my *maybe* to my *yes*. There's a split second when he breaches my barrier that the pinch of pain causes me to flinch and tense. "Shiloh..." he breathes, stilling.

I clasp him to me tightly, my heels finding purchase in his buttocks, and as he is unmoving, afraid to cause me pain, I move for us, breath hitching as I try to convey with my body what I need. I tilt my hips upward and into his, circling and rotating until he groans in defeat. His eyes close and he drops his forehead to mine, beginning to move in earnest, deep, rhythmic thrusts punctuated by words.

"Love you, Shiloh. You...only. You...God..." His words tumble into incoherence. The brief twinge of pain has already eased and smoothed into something different. A sweet tension where we connect, ratcheting upwards. It's a wanting, a demand for something different. Something more.

"Don't stop," I mutter.

With a groan, he pulls almost all the way out, and then drives back into me over and over, the words he chants a benediction and a curse in my ear.

I'm drowning in sensation, waves of pleasure throbbing through me and building...building. The world's spinning on its axis as I careen towards my finish, reaching for it with every sense. Reaching between us, Gunner applies the perfect amount of pressure to my clit, shattering and sending me spiraling. He follows with a hoarse shout immediately afterwards, collapsing and rolling to the side with me tucked into his shoulder.

We lie there, regaining our breath and feeling our heartbeats resume their normal rhythm as the sweat dries and cools on our bodies. I wonder if he can feel the satisfaction radiating through me. After several minutes he sits up and rifles around in the basket near the front of the truck bed, eventually coming back with a towel in hand.

Oh. A muscle ticks in his jaw and I realize that he's upset. I start to sit up and take it from him, but he quietly says, "Let me," and then carefully presses the cloth between my legs. "Did I hurt you?"

"Are you mad at me?" I ask instead.

"No!" He flings the cloth aside. "I'm mad at myself, Shy. I didn't want to hurt you." With jerky motions he pulls his boxer briefs back on.

I tug him back down beside me and cover us both with the quilted blanket. "Gunner. Stop it. I loved it. All of it. You didn't hurt me." I place tiny kisses on his jaw and work my way down to his neck, my hand on his abs making soothing motions. "It's not supposed to feel fabulous the first time."

Some of the tension drains out of him, and he kisses the top of my head. "I wish I'd been able to make it fabulous."

"If you'd made it any better, I'd be dead, Gunner." I look at him dryly. "And it wasn't that painful. Just a pinch."

He looks at me askance. "Maybe for my ego you can say I split you wide open. And maybe walk a little funny tomorrow?" I snort and poke him, and he pulls me tighter into his side. "I don't think I ever asked you. Why were you waiting?"

I shrug. "Honestly? No real reason. The guys I dated in high school were tools. I knew enough to know I didn't want to give that to them; figured they'd be spouting off about it in the locker room the next day. Freshman year of college wasn't much better. And then everything happened at the start of sophomore year with the accident...my life and priorities just took an entirely different turn. I didn't have the time or energy to chase after guys or let them get close enough for any kind of relationship."

Studded with stars, the night sky seems like a weighted blanket upon us as I explain. It settles over us, thick and eternal, reminding me of another sky, another night just like this, except my friend, Cotton, lay beside me. That was the night I kissed Gunner, back when he was a fifteen-year-old freshman and I was just about to turn eighteen, a senior on her way out the door. I look at Gunner's profile and marvel at our beginning—seven minutes in heaven that's turning into something real. "I guess I'm finally at the point where I'm ready for that relationship."

Gunner turns his head and looks at me, pulls me closer to him. "No. You're just finally ready for me." He places his finger on my shoulder and trails it in a looping pattern that tickles faintly but feels good. It takes me a while to realize he's not just making random circles and loops on my skin. He's writing. He writes my name. He writes his own. He draws a heart, and a house.

A faint smile upon my lips as I nestle into the warmth of his body, I concede that he may be right. I have no clue where this guy came from or how I lucked out, but I'm thankful he's here beside me. Loving me.

20
Him

THE BINOCULARS ARE COLD WHERE THEY'RE PRESSED AGAINST MY FACE. In the dark, I can just make out their forms in the truck bed below, pale against the darker tones of the blankets the sap piled in the back. Rising. Falling. Fucking.

My fingers tighten around the binoculars and the image distorts. Carefully, I loosen my grip and recalibrate until it's corrected, continuing to watch until they finish and settle themselves.

Whore.

Once again, I was too slow. I'd been right there, right around the back of the house and ready to make my move. I didn't have to contend with that dipshit dog, had planned everything down to the last detail. With some minor mischief at the vineyard, I ensured she was alone. Sent the text, so she would know I hadn't forgotten her.

I didn't realize little lover boy would arrive so quickly.

Unbidden, I recall an old cartoon I used to watch together. *Curses, foiled again.* I hated that stupid show.

My lip curls and rage trembles through me, a torrent of emotion that reminds me of past wounds and injuries suppressed. I shudder with the insult and fling the binoculars away. This isn't about *her.*

I stare blindly down at the truck in the midst of the vines and feel like screaming. I want to wrap my hands around her slender neck and tighten, until her lips turn blue and capillaries bloom in her eyes. She's giving away what isn't hers to give. She belongs to me, damn her.

I'm not even that angry with the boy. He merely took what was offered. What man wouldn't? She beckoned, and he came running, tongue hanging out like some cartoon cat on the prowl.

No…it's her. That Jezebel, prancing about with her big hazel eyes and her fuck-me mouth. Her sweet ass and her pitiful sob story. Making men trip all over themselves to love her, but does she care?

No.

It's clearly a game to her. I see it so clearly now. She smiles, but she smiles at us all, doesn't she? Shakes her ass for anyone. I thought she smiled for me. Danced for me. I was so wrong about her.

There's a dull ache in my chest, the burn of tears in my eyes. Why does her betrayal hurt so much?

Filthy harlot.

I shut the door to my car without a sound, settling myself in the seat and staring into the darkness to think. This doesn't really need to change anything. Not really. I would have set her on a pedestal, would have revered her before now. That's the key difference. She won't be cherished in the same way, of course, but she'll still be mine.

In some ways, this is better. It allows me license to handle her as a woman ought to be handled. My cock twitches just thinking about it.

I've let her go unpunished for too long. She needs to understand that there are rules, and the rules cannot be broken. When the rules are abandoned, things happen that aren't necessarily fun.

Not for her, anyway. They're quite fun for me.

I tap my finger against my lip as I ponder. But how to accomplish all of this, and swiftly? My patience is wearing thin. And while I do understand his base impulses, this boy needs to understand that he can't touch what's mine. I need to teach him a lesson, as well.

I think for a few minutes, until the perfect idea comes to me. It's guaranteed to send a message, and Shiloh, with her pretty conscience, won't be able to stand it. She'll leave.

And I'll be waiting.

21
Gunner

IT'S THE SOUND OF CRACKLING THAT FIRST INFILTRATES MY SLEEP, along with an insidious, muted roar that my subconscious tries to flee from. My eyelids flutter against a flickering orange light, and part of me wonders if it's morning already.

Then the smell hits me, and I wake fully with a surge of motion, sitting swiftly upright and dislodging Shiloh. She jerks awake and shoves herself sleepily upright. "What's…? Oh, dear God." Her choked exclamation is an echo of my silent one.

I'm already shoving my legs into my jeans, tossing her clothes to her as I see them. "Get dressed. Hurry."

There is no time to waste.

The vines—trellises, really—are burning around us. Even as I grab my phone and race to the cab, opening the door and ensure that Shiloh's in before seating myself, my eyes are searching for the best exit route. We have some space to maneuver and thankfully it snowed just the other day, so the vines are not dry kindling, but the wood trellis frames might as well be a strip of fuel-rigged dominoes, the way the flames lick from one to the next.

I toss the phone to Shiloh. "Call 911." Dimly I hear her doing so as I plow as quickly as I can through the vines that are not aflame, the truck bouncing wildly over the rutted ground.

On the horizon ahead, fire glows a brilliant orange-red, plumes of smoke rising hazy above the hills. The vines spread beneath it, some ablaze as the fire creeps closer, others as yet untouched. I can't make out the source, can't make out the impetus for this hell.

Beside me, Shiloh is tense and silent. She trembles, and if I didn't need both hands to steer, I'd reach over and take her hand. "It'll be all right, Shy. I got you." She doesn't reply.

Finally, we're out of the warren of vines and trellises and at the top of the hill. Sirens sound in the distance, and I brake a safe enough distance away to sit and watch as they come rolling in, passing by us without pause to salvage whatever they can. I can't fathom the destruction in front of me. There is no question in my mind that the fire was deliberately set. It hasn't been dry enough for one to start spontaneously.

Shiloh lifts the console and slides across to me, climbing into my lap to sit pressed up against the door. I move the seat back to give her a little more room and put my chin down on her shoulder.

"I'm so sorry, Gunner," she says, winding an arm around my neck. "The barrels...this. Is it going to hurt the vineyard?"

"These are our oldest vines, so we were considering replanting next season, anyway. He only got to two barrels before Micah showed up. We'll be okay, as long as nothing else on the property has been damaged." I kiss her shoulder. "We just really need to get this guy."

"Not that I want there to be multiple psychos, but are you sure it's him? Could it be anyone, anything else?"

"Not that I can think of. Only one crazy person that I'm aware of, and no other reason for a vineyard to suddenly catch fire in the middle of the night. Especially not at this time of year." Her face falls. "It's not your fault, Shiloh."

"Maybe not directly."

"Not in any way." She moves back to the seat but keeps the armrest tucked away so she can lean against me. We don't talk as we watch the blaze, until I catch sight of a truck in my rearview. "There's Dad."

I watch as his truck pulls alongside mine, both of us rolling our windows down.

"You kids okay?"

"Yessir." I nod.

"Any idea how the hell this happened?" Dad is furious, I can tell from the muscle jumping in his jaw, but he contains it well.

Shiloh turns her head, and from the barely discernible hitch in her breathing I know she's working to keep tears from spilling. Blaming herself, I know.

I shake my head. "Shiloh and I fell asleep in the truck bed down there." I point to a spot almost dead center of the field. "Woke up to fire. If I had to guess, I'd say it's the crazy who's been stalking her."

Dad's lips thin and he faces forward. I see him swallow before he turns back to me. "I'm just glad you woke up. God, when I think…" He shakes himself. "And that's kind of what I figured. I'm going to have a personal chat with the chief, see if we can't get some movement on this. I'd have thought they'd have taken care of this by now." I nod. "Y'all head on back to the house now. Your *nonna's* worried." He rolls his window up and continues toward the activity.

I roll my own up and tug Shiloh to me. "Hey. I know what's going on in that head and it needs to stop."

"This wouldn't have happened if it weren't for me, Gunner. If I'd just listened to that damn text—"

"That's bullshit and you know it."

She subsides into stubborn silence, but I know I haven't convinced her of anything.

"Gunner, do you realize this means he saw us?" I try to keep my expression impassive, but yes, the thought crossed my mind. I tell her so.

"The thought of him watching us…it sickens me." She expels a shaky sigh.

Silence fills the cab, the sounds of the blaze and the shouts of the firemen barely penetrating our little bubble. I don't know what to say to make her feel better, especially right now, at this moment, when it feels like a piece of me is about to shatter. This is my home. That fucker violated me in the one of the most personal ways possible, walking right onto my land and marking his territory. He watched, secure in his anonymity, while Shiloh and I made love for the first time. He watched, and he plotted, and then he set fire to a piece of me.

There's no part of me that isn't certain that it's Shiloh's stalker. I'm not an idiot, and it would be entirely too coincidental for the vines to catch fire around us after we'd made love.

It's him. I know it. I just need to figure out who he is.

Shiloh doesn't wait for me to voice another useless platitude. Instead, she sets her jaw and moves back into the passenger seat, pulling the seatbelt across her hips. "Let's go check on Nonna and Esme," she says. "Let them know what's going on. They're bound to be worried."

Pulling her hand into mine, I restart the truck and head back towards the main house.

Shiloh |

I DIDN'T THINK I'D GO BACK TO SLEEP WHEN I RETURNED TO THE POOL HOUSE, but I did, exhausted by the night's events, I guess. I laid down on the floor by the bed, not wanting to mess up the sheets but needing to stretch out the kinks for a few minutes, and my next conscious moment arrived with sunlight streaming in through gauzy white curtains. I stretch myself awake, stiff and cramped after sleeping on the floor.

Easing myself up, I look to see if Gunner came back from the main house, but he's not here. Things were a mess when we returned, with Nonna and Esme upset and frightened. Nonna had known we were going to be in the vineyard last night and was on the verge of leaving to find us, herself, when we arrived. I crept out around four in the morning, feeling like an interloper. Worse, feeling responsible.

All of this was my fault. If this guy wasn't fixated on me, there'd be no bruises on Gunner. His truck would be fine. His home would be okay. I don't know what I did, or said, but I wish I could go back and erase it.

Heartsick, I go into the bathroom and twist the taps to start the shower, checking for the right temperature before shucking my sooty clothes off and leaving them in a pile on the floor. Looking around for a towel, a flash of black lace catches my eye.

In a set of built-in shelving beside the sink, towels are rolled and stacked. Tucked half in, half out of a basket containing socks and underwear on one shelf, a scrap of lingerie teases me. Pulling it loose, I curl my fingers around the bra I wore for my sexy teacher dance ages ago. The one I tossed to Gunner.

He saved the damn thing.

He *feels* so much. Loves so openly, so hard. It slays me.

Stepping into the glass and tile enclosure, I close the door behind me and let the water sluice over me, washing away last night's grime. I turn and face the wall, letting it beat against my back, and place my forehead against the cool tiles.

I'm going to have to leave. The thought is a dull ache in my chest, a knowledge weighting me down. I'm going to have to break his heart, and mine, too, to keep him and his family safe.

And I'm going to have to do it after telling him with my words, and actions, and body that I trusted him.

That I was done running.

Done hiding.

Done being scared.

And I am. I'm every one of those things. I do trust Gunner, and I am finished running and hiding and being terrified of my feelings. But I'm terrified, now, for him. I couldn't live with myself if anything happened to him.

He's going to hate me. With a shaking hand, I reach out for the bottle of body wash, only to have it plucked gently from my fingers.

Gunner.

At some point he stepped into the shower, and I was so lost to my grief I didn't even notice. I glance back at him over my shoulder and if he sees the desolation I'm sure is written all over my face he doesn't mention it. He doesn't say anything, just squirts soap in his hands and begins stroking it slowly, sensuously over my body.

He starts with my shoulders, thumbs applying firm pressure that straddles the line between pleasure and pain. I let out a groan and start to drop my arms, but he raises them back up and places my hands flat on the wall, massaging the soap into my flesh as he does. "Stay."

Then he's moving down, fingers and palms gliding over every inch of exposed flesh from tip to toe. He traces the curves of my breasts, learning their shape and weight with first a single forefinger and then both hands, before rolling and tugging the nipples between thumb and forefinger. Then he gently massages down my belly, which contracts and flexes with every stroke, helpless under his onslaught.

He brings his hands up along my flanks, pulling me briefly back against him before he steps back, allowing me to feel his hard length against me. Then his fingers are on my ass, exploring every divot and crease with tender fascination. They cup the bottom of my cheeks, dangerously close to that one spot he hasn't touched yet. If I arch just a bit...

"Stop that." With a light chuckle, he moves his hands, trailing them instead to my thighs and spreading me wider.

"Please, Gunner."

"Please what, Shy?"

"I need you—"

With one last stroke up and down my legs, Gunner touches my core, dipping a single finger shallowly into me. I rock against him, a small cry leaving my lips. "Jesus, you're soaking wet." He thrusts another finger into me, plunging both deep this time.

"Stop teasing me, Gunner—"

He replaces his fingers with his cock then, thrusting into me in one sure stroke, and I shudder at the sensation, so primed I am from his attentions. "Wait for me," he whispers. I dance on the razor's edge, struggling to hold myself back from the promised release.

"I can't…" Tears are seeping from the corners of my eyes and I don't know if they're from the orgasm I'm chasing or from the certainty that I have to leave this beautiful man. Abandon this love.

"Come then," he orders, and I do, unraveling entirely like a skein of my cotton wool, legs shaking as I whisper his name, and then secrete it away in the furthest corner of my heart.

Seconds later, he follows me, both of us collapsing to the floor of the shower as we finish to huddle there, breath soughing and hearts racing as we try to recover the unrecoverable.

22
Gunner

"SHILOH." It feels like a roar but the word slips out as a rasp. She's gone.

This has to be some kind of a bad joke. I knew something was off in the shower—damnit, I could see it in her eyes. but this. She had one foot already out the door, was apologizing with one breath and taking what she needed one last time with her next.

But she was grieving the loss. I could see that, had known it as surely as I knew my own name. So why? It doesn't compute.

Anger riding me hard, I skim the dear John letter Shiloh left for me a second time, just to see if it makes more sense than it did the first time I read it.

> *Gunner—*
>
> *I'm sorry. I know this is a cop out, and I know I'm a coward* (damn straight, dolcezza), *but I can't do this. I can't stand by and watch this guy destroy you and your family and everything they've spent generations building. I won't do it.*
>
> *And I knew if I waited...talked to you...you'd tell me everything would be*

okay, and we'd figure it out, and we were worth the risk. And I'd end up believing you.

But Gunner. I'm not sure that's true. What if he comes after Esme? Or Nonna? What if he actually hurts you, instead of your truck or your home? I couldn't live with myself.

I don't expect you to forgive me. I know I just told you no take-backs, and here I am. Running. I won't stop hoping, though, and praying, that one day, when this psycho is caught, that you'll find it in your heart to love me again.

Because I love you, Gunner. So much I'll risk your heart, but not your safety. Please try to understand.

Shiloh

It figures that she'd tell me she loves me in the same breath she tells me she's leaving.

I ball the note up and throw it in the trash, and then, pissed beyond all reason, I pick up the trash can and slam it against the wall. The stainless steel makes a satisfying clang, the wall takes a dent, and the floor is trashed.

"Fuuuuck!" I drop the can and kick it, sending it flying across the room.

Grabbing my phone, I tap in the number for the spare phone I gave Shiloh when I took hers to Twiggy to have it checked over. I don't expect her to answer, but I still feel defeated when it goes straight to voice mail. Defeated, and angry. I thought we were past all this shit. I text her, instead.

> Me: Why won't you talk to me.

Silence. I get myself dressed, attempt patience in case she isn't tethered to her phone. I know that's not the case, though. I try again. Nothing.

> Me: Damnit, Shiloh. Answer.

This time three dots flicker a response. I wait, watching the dots fade in and out, and wonder if she's writing a goddamn book. Then they disappear altogether.

> Me: If you don't talk to me, I'm coming to your house and we're hashing this out face to face.
>
> Shiloh: I won't be here. Don't come, Gunner.
>
> Ah. There she is.
>
> Me: A fucking note, Shiloh?
>
> Shiloh: I explained that. I don't know what else you want me to say.
>
> Me: How about something real?

I'm tired of this bullshit texting and Facetime Shiloh. Once again, she refuses to answer the phone.

> Me: Pick up the goddamn phone.

> Shiloh: I can't.

> Me: Face to face, then.

> Shiloh: Damn it, Gunner.

Taking that as the unwilling acquiescence it is, I call again. This time she answers. She's in her house, in her bedroom from what I can see. She's laying on a pillow and immediately obvious is the fact that she's been crying. Her face is red and blotchy, her eyes bloodshot and puffy. I observe her without speaking for a minute, my eyes devouring her face.

"What?" she finally barks, wiping her nose with a raggedy looking tissue she's clenching in her fist.

"I called to yell at you. To tell you how you're breaking my heart and ask you how you can be so cruel. To remind you how you told me no more running. No more hiding. All in, Shiloh. I called to remind you of that." Tears stream unchecked down her face. "But you look fucking miserable. I'm having a hard time yelling at you."

There's an audible gulp and I see her throat move. "Yell at me, Gunner. I need you to yell, so I won't feel like this."

"How do you feel?"

She inhales, a long, shuddering breath like she's about to say something, but abruptly stops, averting her eyes and shaking her head.

"Do you feel like there's this big, gaping wound in your chest, Shiloh?"

"Stop."

"Do you feel like you're in a fucking nightmare that you can't wake up from?"

"Please. Stop."

"Do you feel like you can't breathe? Like you might never breathe again? 'Cause that's how I feel *dolcezza*. Like you punched your hand right into my chest and ripped out my heart, and then my lungs, and now I'm just waiting—"

"Stop it!"

I stop, and the only sounds are her broken weeping. Finally, she calms herself enough to speak.

"I didn't...I don't know what else to do." Hopelessness is heavy in her tone, and part of me despises her for how easily she gave up.

"You come to me, Shiloh. We deal together. That's what people that love each other do."

"But your family—"

"Is family. And family protects family."

She's shaking her head in denial. "That may be true in most instances, but you can't make that decision for them. We never know when this guy is coming, or from where. We don't know anything except he's starting to get dangerous. I can't believe you'd even consider putting Nonna or Esme at risk."

"I'd never risk them."

"But that's exactly what you're doing if I come back."

I hate that she's mostly right. I can't protect against an enemy I can't see coming.

"Okay. Say you're right. Why don't I come and stay with you at your house? We'll move the target."

"No! It doesn't matter where we are. If we're together, you're still a target. And so is your family. He can still use them to get to me. I'd rather not give him the means."

"Damnit, Shiloh!" Frustrated, I run my hand through my hair. "If you do this..." I don't even know where I'm going with that statement and break off in disgust. I just know my heart is breaking. "Don't do this, Shiloh." Resolve firms her features.

"It doesn't have to be forever. We just... we need to catch this guy." With that, she disconnects, and I'm left staring at a mocking black screen.

23
Shiloh

"I CAN TELL SOMETHING'S WRONG." Cotton's tone makes it clear that she's not letting this go. I refused to turn my camera on for this conversation, not wanting her to see my puffy eyes and red nose. Her call is unexpected, coming through early in the day on Friday rather than Thursday evening as usual.

Probably because I was busy wallowing and elected not to open my laptop or pick up my phone last night. I haven't even gotten out of the bed today, choosing instead a mental health day. Mental health day meaning, gorging oneself on peanut butter cups and TikTok videos.

"I told you, I'm fine." *It's just been almost two days without Gunner and my heart hurts.* "I was busy yesterday."

"Did you go see Sammy?" Yes, and had to suffer through the third degree, because there was no hiding that face. It had been ridiculous, with Sammy glaring at me until I confessed what was going on and Dr. Adams trying to get me to stay overnight at Thurston House.

"We can make up a bed for you in the room right across the hall," he told me, which of course made Sammy throw a minor fit when I refused.

"Yes. We ate Thanksgiving dinner made for the residents."

There's a long pause. "See, this is what I mean. You're skimping on details. Normally you'd say, 'and it was good.' But now you're giving me bare bones, like you're just waiting until you can get off the phone."

Groaning, I throw a pillow off the bed to the floor. "All right, Cotton, you asked for it. I wanted to spare you the drama, but you're so damn..." Words fail me.

"Persistent? Intuitive? Full of love for my best friend? Shiloh, I would bet money right now that you are getting sick off of Reeses right now and still in your pajamas."

"And your point is?" My tone is lofty. I am above this inquisition. Cotton doesn't answer. "Cotton? You there?" I hear the change in volume as the call goes to speaker, the sound of chatter in the background, and I know she's still there. "You're giving me the effing silent treatment, aren't you." It's not a question. This is Cotton's go-to move when something isn't working out quite as she planned. She's bullheaded enough to outlast anybody.

"I could hang up," I threaten. Somebody laughs and a door slams. "Damnit, Cotton. Fine, you win. Short version only. My stalker..." I have to pause for a second, think about how to describe the situation without unduly worrying Cotton. Finally conceding there is no good way, I continue. "Things are getting out of hand. He threw a rock through my window. He videoed me in the bath. He set Gunner's vineyard on fire."

"What!"

"Short version," I remind her. "I left him, Cotton."

"Shiloh." Sympathy screams at me in her tone. "Why?"

I flop back on the bed and stare at the ceiling. "I had to. That crazy fuck set the vineyard on fire while we were down there, sleeping in Gunner's truck."

"Um, what? That needs explanation, I think, but I'll come back to it. Why did he set the vineyard on fire?"

"This goes to your earlier question, but I'm pretty sure he saw Gunner and I doing the deed."

"Oh, my God! You did it! You lost your v-card!"

"Least of my worries, Cotton."

"And outside! Girl!"

I pull the phone away from my ear. "I can hear every single exclamation point, Cotton."

"I'm just so proud of you. You kinky bitch."

"Outside is not kinky."

"Well, it's certainly not staid and respectable. But anyway. So, he saw you two getting jiggy with it, got fired up about it, and...er, fired up."

My sigh is my answer.

"Okay, sorry. That was bad. But why did you leave Gunner? I'm not getting it. Shouldn't you be sticking close to him right now?"

"He sent me a text after Gunner's accident, told me to ditch him or else. This fire was the 'or else.' I can't take the chance that he'll escalate any further and hurt Gunner or his family. The vineyard is bad enough."

"What about another friend? Then Gunner would be appeased, and you would still be safe. I don't like the idea of you being in that house by yourself."

"I'd still be worried the stalker would go after whoever I was with to get to me."

"I kind of hate the logic of that. How did Gunner take it?"

"Not well. He was so upset, Cotton." I close my eyes, not wanting to recall the break in his voice. The anger. "I hurt him."

Cotton's voice is carefully devoid of emotion when she replies. "But you told him everything you told me, right?"

"Of, course, I did! I wasn't going to let him think I didn't love him."

Shit. I hadn't meant to say that.

"You love him."

I draw in a deep breath, release it. "Yeah. I guess I do."

Calm fills me, and I climb from the bed, make my way into the kitchen. Coffee. I need coffee. I know now, with a certainty that comes from new clarity, that I did the right thing. Gunner may never forgive me. He may never want me back.

But at least he'll be safe.

24
Shiloh

Gunner: still tutoring me, or bailing on that, too? I have a paper due at end of week.

GUNNER'S TEXT PINGS AS I WALK INTO KENDRICK'S for my shift Monday afternoon. I sigh and pocket my phone.

My heart hurts at the anger and pain he doesn't trouble to hide in the message. I wish I could rewind, erase everything that's happened in the past couple of days. That wouldn't make what I'm doing now less justified, though. I know I'm doing the right thing. Gunner knows it, too. He just doesn't want to admit it.

Closing my eyes in the doorway that leads from the back to the bar, I count slowly to ten. Let it go, I tell myself. Deal with your shift, then deal with Gunner.

It proves difficult to do so, though.

Twenty minutes into my shift, Gunner sits in his usual spot. Breaking things off with him apparently did nothing as far as having him follow me around; he was making his presence felt whether I liked it or not.

As I slice lemons and limes for drinks, I look up at him from across the expanse of bar and club. He meets my eyes, takes a long sip of his drink, and tips the brim of his ball cap at me.

I don't mistake the gesture for manners. Gunner is mad, and this is how he shows it.

I pause in my task and push my glasses back into position on the bridge of my nose.

If I do so with my middle finger, well...no one noticed but Gunner. His face darkens with a scowl.

"What's up with all that?" Teddy comes to stand beside me and nods toward Gunner. "I thought you guys were a thing."

Oops. I guess someone else was paying attention. "We're on a little break," I tell him.

"And Ford's not too happy, I take it? Why's he here?"

I contemplate his question as I slice another lemon. There's no real reason to keep my problem a secret. It might even be better for more people to know. It'd mean more eyes, anyway.

"I have a stalker," I tell him baldly. "No idea who, but some certified crazy person is having himself a time fucking with me."

"You have a fucking stalker?" Before I can answer he starts moving to serve a customer. "Hold on. I want to hear more." He's back in a minute. "Okay, hit me with it."

So, I do. Teddy is surprisingly easy to talk to, listening with only the occasional interjection or question. A frown wrinkles his forehead, deepening when I finish telling him about the fire, leaving out the catalyst for it.

"So, contact between Gunner and me is not a good idea at the moment."

"So, you're just calling it quits for a while?"

"Wouldn't you? It sucks on several levels, though, not the least of which is the fact that I am legitimately tutoring and trying to help him graduate. That's why he's over there glowering. He sent me a text earlier telling me he has an assignment due on Friday that he needs my help with."

Teddy says nothing at first. In fact, I'm beginning to think I rendered him speechless when he tosses the towel he was using to dry glasses to the bar and turns to me.

"You've gone to the police?"

"Yes, of course."

"And they're not helping?"

"It's not that they're not helping. It's more that they're doing everything they can, and it's still not good enough."

"They're that good, huh?"

"They?"

"He? She? Do you really know? 'They' seemed like a safe bet."

I shrug. "Yeah, I guess. I can't imagine it's a woman, though."

"What are the police doing?"

"The usual stuff. Checking regularly for listening and recording devices. Frequent drives by the property. Investigation of all physical evidence, of which there's not much." He nods and I continue. "I just don't understand, why me? From both the poor, pitiful me standpoint and the what the heck is so special about me standpoint. And I've been racking my brain over everyone I know, and I can't think of anyone who would do something like this to anyone."

"Most people have hidden depths you never know about."

"I guess. Still waters, and all that."

At that moment, a glass thunks on to the bar between us. "What are you two discussing so intently?" Gunner asks, gaze fixed in challenge on Teddy.

I move his glass and grab a new one. "Refill?" Without waiting on an answer, I scoop ice into it.

"We were just talking about Shiloh's stalker problem," Teddy says. "Sounds like it's putting a cramp in your style.

"We'll figure it out," I say, sliding Gunner's drink his way.

"I don't see why you couldn't at least meet with me in a public place to do the tutoring," Gunner says. "Like a library or something?"

"Are you kidding? If we're in a public place, it's that much easier for this guy to see us!" I can't believe him.

"My point, exactly. If he sees we're not doing anything but school stuff, he should be appeased, right? Maybe he'll back off."

"Gunner, he already knows we're doing more than tutoring."

"We're not doing anything anymore, isn't that right?" He turns that challenge my way. "I could even bring Esme with me. It's worth a shot, right?"

I look at Teddy, who's been observing in silence. "I don't know. What do you think?"

He shrugs, picks up his dishtowel. "I plead the fifth."

3:30 PM. The conference room in the library is cramped and sterile looking, with a small office table, a white board on the wall, and not much else. Since I left a note for Gunner and Esme at the desk, letting them know where I'd be, I take a seat and wait.

Esme comes in after a few minutes, slams her backpack down, and drops into a chair across from me. "Gunner's on the way." She stares balefully at me and I sigh, having a good idea of how the next hour is going to go.

"All right, Esme. Clearly you have something you'd like to get off your chest. Hit me with it."

Her eyes, just like Gunner's, are pale chips of ice. "I don't get you, Shiloh. My brother is a catch. And he's spent the last five years mooning over you." She flings up a hand, signaling frustration. "And I know you like him." I almost snort. Like. Yes, Esme…I *like* him quite a lot.

"What did he tell you, Esme?" I interrupt gently.

"Nothing. He won't tell us anything except that you left. And after one of the worst nights of our lives." She trails off, and when she speaks again her voice is small and she refuses to look at me. "Did he…I know you guys had a picnic date that night. Did he do something to upset you?"

"Oh, Esme, no. Your brother is the most amazing man I know. He's good, Esme. Kind, generous, intelligent. He wears his heart on his sleeve. I'd be a fool not to care for him."

Esme's looking at me now, and she sees right through me. "If you love him, then why are you doing this? Why are you breaking his heart like this?"

"I have to, Esme. It has nothing to do with anything he's done, or not done. It has nothing to do with you guys, or anything like that. It's something completely outside of our control."

She's shaking her head, determined to make me see reason. "No. I don't accept that. He's not eating, Shiloh. I don't think he's sleeping, either. And he's just plain mad, all the time."

"Esme." I grab hold of her hand. "Listen to me. Gunner didn't tell you everything that was going on, probably because he wants to protect you. But I'm responsible for the arson at the vineyard. It's my fault."

Esme looks at me in horror, and I realize she thinks I mean I set the fire. I rush to set her straight. "No—I don't mean I set the fire. I mean it's because of me, because of my presence, that someone started it." Confusion has Esme crinkling her brow. "I have a stalker, Esme. We've been trying to figure out who it is, trying to escape from his obsession, for weeks now, but he just keeps moving closer. The fire was the last straw. I can't risk him deciding the best way to get to me is through you, or Nonna, or Gunner. He's already gone after him once—"

Esme gasps. "His truck?" I nod.

The small room is silent for a while as Esme processes. Finally, she looks back at me. "I get it," she says. "I don't like it, but I get it."

I release the breath I hadn't realized I was holding. "Thank you," I say. "If it makes any difference, when all of this is over and there's no longer any risk to you or anyone else, I'll still be here. My feelings won't change. I can only hope he'll still want me."

"Shiloh…" She looks at me sadly. "I said I get it. Not that I agree with it. I imagine my brother feels the same way. If you can't trust him to handle things when times are tough, why would he give you his good times?"

I stare, jaw agape, at her blunt wisdom. There's a pressure behind my eyes warning of tears and I bite it back. Is she right? For the first time I consider that I may have screwed this up beyond redemption, and although I fought against it initially, I really, really want this thing with Gunner. My chest hurts, and I rub the heel of my hand against it, trying to ease the sudden tightness.

"I…I'll be back. Tell Gunner to come and find me if he comes in." I excuse myself and make my way to the stacks.

They rise up tall, heavy wooden shelves reaching for the ceiling, and extend row upon row to the back of the building. The comforting scent of books wraps itself around me as I stride to the furthest corner, intent on a moment of privacy. Finding an empty stack, I lean my head forehead against the wood shelf and close my eyes. *If you can't trust him when things are tough, why would he trust you with his good times?* The words echo in my mind.

Although I'd considered the idea that leaving would be a breaking point for Gunner, I don't think I ever fully believed I'd outrun his feelings for me. Esme knows him, though, a hundred times better than I do. We both know his heart. She also knows his pride. His stubbornness.

The extent to which he can be pushed before he pushes back or walks away.

I can't escape the sinking feeling that says I may have really messed up.

Just then a whisper of sensation ghosts across my nape, and I feel my hair stir. A pair of arms, the sleeves rolled up along forearms dusted with dark hair and corded with muscle, settle on either side of the shelves in front of me, and the scent of sandalwood wraps itself around me. I don't open my eyes, simply let my head fall back until it rests against his chest, and sigh.

"We can't do this."

Gunner doesn't say anything at first. He bends his face into the tousle of hair at my neck and inhales, then slowly exhales. His breath, hot on my skin, tickles my nerve endings. I shiver, and he chuckles without humor, low in my ear. Restless, I shift, pressing my thighs together at the involuntary wash of heat that suffuses me.

"Still being stubborn?"

"I have to. Gunner—"

"Shh. I like this skirt you're wearing."

Lips burn a lazy path down my neck and push aside the wide neck of my sweater to continue across my shoulder. I start to turn around, needing to put an end to this.

"Stay." He positions me back as I am, moving my hands to the shelf above me.

"You're being very bossy," I say as his hands make a leisurely journey down my body.

"You like it." I don't have the will to deny the truth of his statement, especially when he drags a hand under the hem of my skirt and cups me between my legs. Instead, it drags a low moan from between my lips, and his fingers squeeze, his middle finger pressing firmly against my clit. When I start to move, restless, he kicks one leg out a few inches with his foot and presses me against the stacks, leaving no room for movement. "Be still."

I feel him shifting behind me, lowering himself, and chance a look down to see him lifting my skirt with his free hand. "Wha—what are you doing? You can't do this here."

"You don't give me much choice," he says roughly. "We're not done just because you say so. Now be quiet, *dolcezza*." With those words, he pulls my underwear free with a stinging snap of the elastic, spreads my folds, and licks my seam. Stifling a cry, I hold on to the stacks and shake as he slides his tongue deep inside me, followed by two fingers. His words echo through me, loosening the tightness in my chest. *Not done*.

Angling his head just right and pushing on my lower back to impose an exaggerated arch, he sucks my clit into his mouth and tugs.

"Shiloh? I saw Gunner." Esme's loud whisper echoes through the area.

"Shit…." I breathe, while Gunner smiles into my pussy. "Coming," I manage, and then I am, biting on my hand to muffle the cry that emerges. I sense Gunner moving away and rising to his feet and straighten myself out as best I can before I turn to face him.

"Was that to prove some kind of point?" I ask, meeting his gaze. His eyes are cold and yet they burn. He turns to walk away. "Gunner—" He stops, and I swallow. "—my panties?"

"Are mine," he finishes brusquely. Without a backward look, he walks away, leaving me standing in the stacks, bare-assed and fighting tears.

25
Shiloh

IT'S FUNNY HOW THINGS ALWAYS SEEM TO COME IN GROUPS—threes, usually. First my job. Then Gunner's accident. Then the fire. Now I've just sat down to a Skype call with Cotton a week after the fire when a text notification buzzes through and a knock sounds on the door. I roll my eyes. "Hang on a sec," I tell Cotton, glancing at the text. It's Gunner. I start to reply when the knock comes again, more insistent, and set it down to deal with later. "Someone's at the door."

Leaving the laptop open on the coffee table, I move around to open the door. As I swing it open, belatedly I remember Gunner's aggravation when I did so with him, without first checking the peephole. Everything—every stinking little thing—reminds me of him these days.

Especially since our little interlude in the library. I still can't believe he did that in a public place. I can't believe I let him.

Dr. Adams stands on the porch, hands in pockets. He's wearing a smile and a casual sweater under a barn jacket; his legs covered in denim.

"Dr. Adams. What are you doing here?" Surprise is evident in my voice and I know my question is rude, but I can't help it. He's never come to my home before. "Is everything all right? Did something happen to Sammy?"

"No, no. I thought we were meeting today? For the home visit? Oh, shoot, did I get the date wrong?"

I rub my forehead, and remembering my manners, step back to let him in. "No, I'm sure you are here exactly when you're supposed to be. I've been forgetting everything lately. Come on in." The doctor enters and glances around at the living room to our right.

"Nice place," he says.

"Thanks." It's weird having him here in my home, away from Thurston House. "Can you remind me what you'll be looking for? Where he'll be doing his physical therapy, bed and bath accessibility—things like that?"

Dr. Adams smiles. "Yes, exactly. Want to give me the nickel tour and I'll take notes as we go?"

"Sure. There's not much to it. I submitted a report detailing the home environment to your facility not too long ago. You can find measurements and stuff on it if you need them."

"Excellent. Having that will make this go much faster."

"Great." I gesture to the living room. "Follow me, then. Obviously, this is the living room." As I look at it through someone else's eyes, I wonder what they see. A small room, comfy, worn furniture. "I plan on storing some of the furniture that's in here to create a more open plan." I think about Cotton sitting on Skype, waiting. She doesn't have a large window of time. I'm sure she can hear what's going on, though. She'll hang around as long as she can.

He has a pen in hand and twirls it between his fingers. He nods as he looks at the living room. "Yes, wider paths in here for sure. You'll need to think about getting rid of that chair, maybe moving the couch forward a few inches." He wanders over to the picture window that I hadn't had replaced yet. "What happened here?"

"Some creep through a rock through my window several days ago." I cross my arms over my chest at the memory.

Dr. Adams' face tightens. "Sheesh. That's not good. Were you here at the time? I bet that was a frightening experience."

I nod. "It was awful." I follow as he winds down the adjacent hall, turning my head so I can catch Cotton's eye on the laptop.

Sorry, I mouth. *Be right back.* She nods and waggles her brows suggestively, as if to say, *not too shabby.* I grin and shake my head. It's almost scary how we can read each other.

"Did you say something?" The doctor asks.

"Oh, no."

He is already opening the door to the hall bathroom and looking in. "The hall is nice and wide, but the bathroom here is a little small," he notes, glancing back at me. "I think it would take fairly extensive remodeling to get it to where it needs to be for Sammy. Is this the one he'll be using, or do you have another?"

"There's the master." I slide past him and lead the way. "I was thinking I'd give him the master bed and bath, and I would take a smaller bedroom. I don't need the big one."

Inside the bedroom, I'm self-conscious as he makes a slow perusal of my messy bed and the few clothes piled on the chair. "Why, Shiloh Brookings. Are you a slob?" he asks teasingly. There's an odd intensity in his expression as his eyes travel the room. Something foreign and unnerving.

"Maybe a little. I completely flaked on anyone coming over today." He doesn't respond. "Bathroom's through here." I push open the door to the bathroom and step inside. "This should be big enough, right?"

Mom had the bathroom remodeled around a year before she died, and it's one of the nicest rooms in the house, with a soaker tub and separate walk-in shower with a glass enclosure. The floor is a hard tile that resembles hardwood but has the benefit of being water insoluble—perfect for a wheelchair. "I think all I'll have to do is put up some rails, maybe?"

Dr. Adams has yet to speak. I turn to find him standing just behind me, entirely too close. He's not even looking at the bathroom, I think with irritation. His eyes are focused on me. I squint. I thought I had made it clear that I was not interested. "Dr. Adams?"

"Shiloh," he breathes, raising a hand to brush against my cheek. "Pretty, pretty Shiloh."

His voice is the first thing that strikes me. It's subtly different, the tone and cadence altered.

I flinch away from his touch and start to back up but realize immediately that I'm only backing further into the bathroom. Grabbing the door, I try to swing it shut, but he's there, in the way. With an easy flick of his wrist he pushes it away from him and follows, making me stumble back until I end up pinned between him and a wall, scant inches dividing us. "What are you doing?" I try to project strength into my words, but they come out all wrong—a small squeak against the thick atmosphere between us.

"Shiloh…" he leans his forehead against mine and I shudder at the sensation of his breath against my face. Something that Gunner does all the time that makes me shiver with delight repulses me with the doctor. It's as if my skin knows the wrongness of that touch, even when my brain failed to recognize it. "I've wanted you for so long. Watched over you. Waited for you. Don't you see it? See me?"

Click. All of the pieces snap into place like a child's set of blocks. It's been him all this time. Not Shane. Not some random, faceless man. Everything makes a terrible kind of sense now. The animosity towards Gunner. The too solicitous way he always spoke to me. The little touches. I should have trusted my instincts. "You're my stalker."

His mouth curves and he strokes a finger along my cheek. "Stalker. Such an ugly word for how I feel for you."

"You've been watching me...spying on me."

"I had to make sure you understood, Shiloh. Had to make sure you didn't veer from the path." His eyes harden, the blue turning icy.

"Doctor." I firm my voice, place a hand on his shoulder and press against it. He doesn't move. "You need to take a step back."

Fanaticism lights his face and he places two strong hands on my shoulders, ignoring me when I try to squirm out of his grasp. "You never saw it, though, did you? Never understood the lengths I went to for you."

"What lengths? What did you do for me?" My cell phone is on the table in the living room. And Cotton. Cotton is on Skype. I need to get him back in there so I can call 911, or at least get close enough for Cotton to hear what's happening. "Why don't we go in the living room? I'll pour us both a glass of tea, and we can sit down and talk this out."

He ignores my words and trails a finger into the cleavage of my top. "You've been a bad girl, Shiloh.

Fucking that boy. Letting him touch you. I'm going to have to purify you now." He tsks.

"I don't want this, Dr. Adams. We're friends. I don't have those kinds of feelings for you." Again I shove, and this time manage to move him a step, enough for me to dart past. I walk swiftly out of the bedroom and down the hall, or at least…that's what I attempt. I'm almost in the living room when he grabs me, his hands bruising on my upper arms as they pull me close to him. As I wrestle within his grip, trying to get loose, I feel the prick of something sharp at my neck, and try to scream. *This isn't happening,* I think dully, as my mind starts to cloud and the room begins to haze.

A shadowy figure stands in the doorway, a blurred silhouette with the sun to his back. "What are you doing to her?" From what seems like miles away, I hear a voice. Familiar, yet strange. I can't…think.

"You don't understand yet, pretty Shiloh," Dr. Adams murmurs, close to my ear and yet it sounds as if it's passing through a tunnel. I think maybe his whisper will be the last sound I hear. "But you will."

DARKNESS. Motion. A strange, rhythmic sound that's a cross between a thump and a whoosh. From a distance, the sound of music. *Sweet Dreams*, by the Eurythmics, I think.

Through the subsiding haze of whatever the doctor drugged me with, I note that it's dark. Pitch black. Am I blindfolded? I try to reach my hands up to feel my face and discover that they're bound before me with some kind of thin plastic strip.

A zip tie, my brain supplies, and I have to push down the fear that surges. Zip ties are what organized, ruthless planners use—or at least, that's what Hollywood has shown. They indicate someone thought about their crime, mapped it out beginning to end. A zip tie is different from a scarf grabbed in haste, or a shoelace at hand. There's no room to shift one's hands or loosen the binding.

I swallow and try to focus. My cheek itches from the rough material it's pressed against, and I feel like I'm going to puke. There's a roiling in my stomach, a by-product, I'm sure, of the constant motion and the drug.

Dr. Adams. Sammy's doctor! A person we trusted…a man who took the Hippocratic oath. Anger and a raw sense of betrayal courses through me but I shove it aside for the time being. Not the time and not the place for uncontrollable emotion. I should focus on what I can do to possibly get away.

I can take stock of my surroundings, even with my hands tied. I kick my feet out, gingerly at first and then with more force as the parameters of my prison crystallize. I'm in the trunk of a car.

Dear God, he's taking me somewhere. First rule of kidnaping—other than don't get kidnaped in the first place—don't let them take you to a different location. I deepen my breathing to quell my rising panic. *In. Out. In. Out.*

It's hard to tell with only my sense of hearing and touch to guide me, but the steady whoosh and thump indicates that we may be on a highway, one of those annoying concrete ones with the seams. The thumps come so rapidly one after another that I have to assume we're moving pretty rapidly.

I calm somewhat as I gather each piece of sensory input and place them together like a puzzle. The taillights. I watched a movie once where the heroine kicked the taillight out of the trunk and the police stopped the driver. Maybe I can try… As the thought forms in my mind, I start to twist and jerk until I'm facing the back of the car, and lifting my hands, try exploring the area in front of me.

I can't feel a taillight. The itchy carpeted lining extends to the seams of the trunk closure. My fingernails scrabble against it, searching for a loose area to pull the lining away. I pinch my eyes closed against the tears of frustration that well. Will it work, anyway? After repositioning myself again, I lift my good ankle and kick. And kick, again. Again.

But it doesn't work. I go limp, sweating despite the chill in the air, and try to think. The back seat. I should be able to kick the back seat out. But I don't want to do that while he's driving. One, I can't go anywhere while we're driving this fast. Two, if I'm able to kick it out after he stops, I may have a second long enough to surprise him. Maybe he'll leave the keys in the ignition, and I can wriggle through and lock the doors, drive away really fast. Or just climb out the back and run.

I wriggle myself into the most proximal position, and after a testing flex of my feet against the back seat, I wait.

I need to free my hands, somehow. This is going to be really fucking hard with them zip tied.

Even though I know it's not likely to accomplish anything, I twist and pull at the plastic strip. I have to try.

Dr. Adams. With nothing immediate I can do, my mind goes back to my captor. I can't believe I've been so stupid blind. That was him in the peep box. He used my brother against me—his own patient. He seemed so genuine, so committed. Maybe it's the drug, but I'm having trouble reconciling reality with not only my predicament, but with the fact that my stalker is a man I've looked up to and respected for years who put me here.

Hot tears sting my cheeks as I wonder when my disappearance will be discovered.

Or if it will be discovered in time.

26
Gunner

I'VE NEVER PUT MUCH STOCK IN THOSE STORIES OF PEOPLE who claim to have some feeling of doom right before something terrible happens. Depending on how this day turns out, though, I might end up changing my attitude. All day I've been unable to shake this sense of heaviness. Portent. And now I can't get Shiloh on the phone.

That, coupled with this sensation, is freaking me out a little, not going to lie.

It could just be the weather. Virginia weather is notoriously fickle, especially in the highlands, and although several days ago it was mild enough to sleep under the stars, today dawned frigid cold and overcast. It's spitting occasional sleet that stings my flesh and reminds me that we have months to go before warm days return.

Anyone might feel a sense of unease on such a nasty day, but I can't shake the feeling that something besides the weather is not right.

I tried texting earlier. Saw those three little dots appear, as if she were composing a reply. Then they disappeared, and that was it. So I tried again. And again. Then I tried calling. I blew her fucking phone up. There's no doubt in my mind that if she were able, Shiloh would reply out of sheer annoyance, regardless of what we have between us right now.

So yeah...I'm a little worried.

I try to curb my fears as I stride into Kendrick's, where she's on schedule to work tonight. I need to tamp down the emotion, because I know it won't accomplish anything for me to go raging around, eyes wild, demanding answers.

I scan the bar first. It's slammed with customers, most of them well-dressed men in suits, ties loose around their necks. It's the end of the workday and they're here to let off steam. Miles's father is a madman in action as he slings drinks and works the tap. I push my way in and slap a hand on the polished wood surface. "Yo, Mr. K."

"Hey, Gunner. What are you doing here? Miles with you?" He stays in motion as he speaks, eyes flickering behind me to look for Miles.

"No, I'm alone. Where's your help?"

His lip curls. "Neither one of them showed up. Both of them, fucking no-shows. What the hell's up with that, Gunner? I did you a solid, giving that girl her job back, putting her behind the bar, and this is how she repays the favor?" He strides to the other end while I bite my tongue. He only knows what's right in front of him.

He returns a few minutes later, stares at me hard. "Do you know where she is? 'Cause I could use a hand here."

"I don't. That's why I'm here." He starts to shake his head and I can tell he's pissed. "But I know this. Shiloh doesn't blow off work."

Kendrick raises an eyebrow as he hands a tray of drinks off to a waitress. "Then where is she? Don't look at me like that, son. Just stating facts."

"Yeah, me too." I turn my back to him and survey the club. I see a few familiar faces, regulars who are always here. A bachelor party is in progress down near the stage.

I turn back to the bar to find Kendrick watching me, arms stretched out on either side of him.

"So what's going on?"

"She's had some trouble with a stalker. That was why I asked Miles to see what you could do with getting her out of the peep. I didn't want her here at all."

He grunts. "She's the sister of that boy who had the accident...Sammy?"

I nod. "I can't get her on the phone. I'm getting a little worried, especially now that I'm here and find out she hasn't called in—"

"Gunner." I turn at the sound of my name and see Shane Reasor at my elbow.

"What the fuck do you want?" I'm in no mood for this dude's foolishness. He takes a step back at my expression before firming his jaw.

"Look, I know what you think of me. It's fine. I deserve it. But I wanted you to know I didn't say a word about where Shiloh worked, or the fact that you two had something going on. That's not my style."

I narrow my eyes at him. "What is your style, Reasor? You stalking her?" I know it's not likely to be Shane, since he's here, but I can't help the question.

He rears his head back like I've punched him. "What? No! I don't stalk girls!"

"What do you call it when you mess with her car and then conveniently show up to save the day?"

Shane holds his hands up. "I don't know what the hell you're talking about. I was driving by that day and saw her on the side of the road. Should I have ignored her?"

A slim tendril of doubt snakes its way in. "You ever book a peep show with her?"

"Hell, no." He pauses. "I've always wanted her to see me, you know? She was always so dismissive. I never understood why. She wouldn't even know it was me in a peep show." Disgust twists his lips. "I'd feel like a fucking creep."

I nod. *If not you, then who?*

I must have said the words out loud, because Shane looks uncomfortable. "That's why I came over here. I heard you asking about her." Pulling out his phone, he swipes to open his texts and holds it out. "You remember her friend, Cotton? We still message from time to time. She just sent this to me."

> Cotton: Shane! I'm worried about Shiloh.
>
> Shane: What's up?
>
> Cotton: Some guy came over while we were Skyping. Shiloh never came back to the call.
>
> Shane: Maybe she got busy, haha. Was it Gunner?
>
> Cotton: No...someone else. I could barely hear, but I think she called him Alan.
>
> Shane: Huh. I'll keep an eye out for her.

Cotton: Thanks. Let me know. Maybe
we should call police?

Shane: Prob ought to give it a little
time. They'd tell us to wait, anyway.

Dread suffuses me. *Alan.* That's got to be Dr. Adams.
I think back to his odd hostility towards me when I
visited Sammy with Shiloh. He tried to conceal it
beneath a veneer of courtesy, but I saw it. The enmity
that one rival holds for another.

I look at Shane. "Ask for Detective Morris. Tell him
Shiloh's stalker is Dr. Jason Adams, and he has Shiloh—
" My phone rings and I glance down at it. Twiggy.
Shane's already dialing the police, so I start striding
toward the exit as I answer.

"Twiggy."

"Gunner, good news. I was finally able to pinpoint
the owner of the phone where that last text message came
from."

"Jason Adams."

"How'd you know? Did something happen?"

"He has Shiloh, Twig. I need you to find that phone
for me. Can you do that? I need to know where to go."

"Shit...where the hell was Brodie? I can do
that...one sec. That's how I figured out it was him. The
location was that fancy therapy residence."

I'm opening the driver's side door when Shane jogs
out behind me and goes to the passenger side. "Let me
help, Gunner." I hesitate. "You don't have any idea of
what you'll be walking into. You might need extra eyes,
extra hands. We might need to split up to look for her."
As he rambles on, I realize that he's right.

"Shit. Get in." I start the engine and secure the phone in its holder before starting to pull out of the lot. "Where am I going, Twig?"

"He's moving, Gunner."

"Towards his practice?"

"No—slightly different direction. Up Claytor Mountain." Inwardly I curse. That's a ways away. I look over at Shane and he's already calling the police to report the location.

"Alright, Twig. We're headed in that direction. See what you can find for me as far as why he's headed way out there." The possibilities make my throat tight. Lots of woods out there. Lots of places to disappear.

"On it."

"And Brodie…we need to find out what happened there."

"Already got it covered. You just drive, Gunner. I'll call you back in a few." She disconnects, and for several minutes there's nothing but the sound of the tires on the road. The quiet notches up my tension. "Fuck!" I slam my fist into the steering wheel, needing to hit something, and the horn makes a sharp burst.

"We'll find her, Gunner. She's only been gone a couple of hours, and we're right behind her." He means well, but I can't listen to that shit right now.

"I shouldn't have let her go," I say, more to myself than Shane. "I opened the door for him."

"It's not your fault, Gunner." Silence falls again, and I drive.

"For what it's worth, I'm sorry I was an ass," I finally tell him. "I thought it was you."

"We're cool." He shifts beside me, offers me a crooked smile. "Let's just find your girl."

27
Shiloh

I MUST HAVE FALLEN ASLEEP, because I wake again from my drug-induced doze to the unmistakable feel of gravel crunching under the tires. We're moving slowly now, and the darkness feels even more profound than it did earlier. Panic wells and I push it down. I can't panic. He might drug me again.

As I'm focusing on breathing deeply in, slowly out, I feel the car shake with the feel of a door slamming. Quickly, I pull my knees up and punch them out toward the back seat. It gives a sluggish shift forward and then back again, but my movement accomplishes nothing except to send a spear of agony through my still-tender ankle. Then there's a rustling at the back of the car, and the click of a lock. The truck opens with a controlled pop, and I look up to see Dr. Adams looming over me. He looks larger in his casual clothing and I can't help thinking that his strength, so necessary for dealing with infirm patients, is not going to be my friend.

"Dr. Adams," I start, hating how breathless I sound. "Why are you doing this?" My eyes burn with tears I refuse to shed. "What about Sammy?"

His face suffuses with ire. "I've told you. *Jason*." He waits for my nod. "Sammy will be fine. As long as you cooperate, that is." He bends and pulls me upward by my forearms. I wince at the painful movement and Dr.—

Jason— chuckles. "Oops. So sorry. Couldn't be helped. Let's get you inside."

He levers me out of the trunk, and I find myself wobbling on my feet, still half in the grip of whatever it was he dosed me with. Ever solicitous, he wraps an arm around my waist and half-drags, half-carries me toward the structure in front of us.

It's a small cabin with a narrow porch fronting it and a green tin roof that blends with the surrounding trees. I frown. I'm pretty sure this is the same cabin I saw when I visited Sammy a while ago. If it is, we've approached from the opposite direction, which means the lake is at its back. Trees are everywhere, their depths dark with the evening and overgrown underbrush.

"Home sweet home," Jason singsongs. His face, from what I can see in the dim light of the moon, is cheerful. I wonder, yet again, how I failed to notice the wrongness gleaming behind those eyes. I wonder if I'm the first girl he's brought here.

I resolve, in that moment, to do whatever it takes to ensure my survival. I'll cater to every mad whim he has if I have to. Play his little game and wait for my chance to escape. If I'm here…this close to Thurston House…Hope wells within me.

"It's…nice," I tell him. "What is this place?"

Jason pulls me up a short flight of wooden plank steps and holds me against him firmly while he unlocks and pushes open the door. "This is my lake house, Shiloh. My little hideaway. This is where I'll conduct your training."

"Training? Training for what?"

The interior of the cabin is spare but clean. To the left there's a small kitchen separated from the main living space by a bar. The living room boasts a tatty-looking plaid sofa, a recliner near the door with a throw draped loosely over the back, and a small stone fireplace against the far wall. A door in the back leads to what I assume is a bedroom. Jason pushes me on to the couch.

"Train you for me, pretty Shiloh. I have very exacting standards." He squats and with a single slice of a pocketknife I hadn't seen coming, cuts through the zip ties binding my wrists tightly together. Sensation in the form of prickles and instant pain wash over me as circulation returns, eclipsing his words momentarily. Biting back a whimper, I try to flex my fingers.

"I don't understand."

"It's very simple." Jason moves into the kitchen. "You're mine now, Shiloh. You have been for a while, but you were being a little dense. I grew tired of waiting for you to figure it out on your own. And you were starting to get a little naughty, weren't you?" His words are teasing but accompanied by a dark edge that makes me clench my teeth. I look away, desperate to process my environment and figure a way out. There are fireplace implements resting on the hearth. If I could move fast enough, wait until his attention is diverted— maybe I could take him by surprise?

Jason's hand is on my throat suddenly, pushing me back into the sofa cushions. I try to suck in a breath and claw at his wrist as black dots swim across my vision. "Lesson one. I ask a question, you answer." Spittle hits my face as he leans in close. "Do you understand?" I blink frantically and he releases my throat, standing and looking down in satisfaction as my eyes stream. "Good. You're a good girl, Shiloh." He uses his thumbs to wipe at the tears beneath my eyes and I close them. He's a psychopath. A bona fide sicko.

"Let's try that again. You've been naughty, haven't you, Shiloh?" I nod carefully. "Words, darling." He leans in close again, so close I can feel his hot breath on my face. He places his hands on the back of the couch next to my head.

"Yes," I whisper. "I've been naughty."

"But you're ready to be a good girl now, is that right?"

I start to nod, remember myself. "Yes, Jason." I can feel him, thick and hard, as he leans against me, pinning me up against the back of the sofa. It makes me sick. I need air, space. "May I use the bathroom?"

At that moment I hear something outside. Tires, crunching on gravel. Jason hears it also and rises swiftly, moving to the window. He pulls the edge of the brown curtain to the side slightly and peers outside, and his mouth curves in a smile. "I have a surprise for you, Shiloh."

There are steps on the porch, and the door opens. "Hello, Shiloh."

Teddy stands in the doorway, looking almost comically as he does at Kendrick's in dark pants and shirt under a plain taupe colored jacket. His expression is what captures my attention and sends my reflexive burst of hope fizzling. He's not at all surprised to see me here.

"Teddy? What...why..." I can't string together the words to form a complete sentence as Teddy shrugs out of a jacket and lays it over the back of the chair. He starts unbuttoning the cuffs of his shirt and folding them up to reveal corded forearms.

He gives me a mirthless smile. "Surprise."

I swing my gaze to Jason to find him bouncing on his toes, glee twisting his features. "She had no idea, Teddy. None." He's almost childlike in his thrill, the change in his normally professional demeanor disturbing. Teddy, by comparison, is intimidating even without physical size. He has a cold, contemplative expression that makes me think he's studying and dissecting everything about me.

And I guess, if he and Jason are here together, that he's been doing exactly that for some time.

I close my eyes and lay my head back against the sofa. "What do you plan to do with me?" I ask quietly. I have a hundred other questions. How do they know each other. Have they done this before. What my fate is, though, seems to be the most critical question.

"She's so calm," Teddy states, a note of wonder in his voice. "So accepting. This is not what I was expecting."

"Now that she knows, she wants to be here," Jason answers. "I told you. She just needed to know."

I feel heat as one of the men nears me and open my eyes to see Teddy squatting beside me, peering inquisitively into my face. "Is that the truth, Shiloh? Do you want to be here? With us?"

His tone is musing, and I think he's more talking aloud than he is asking me for a response. I repeat my earlier question. "May I use a bathroom?"

Jason steps in front of Teddy. "Of course, darling. Come." He extends a hand to me and Teddy rises, letting me pass. I follow him through the door in the back. It is a bedroom, outfitted with an old wood spindle bed covered with a patchwork quilt. The cabin would be cozy, I find myself thinking, if it didn't belong to a couple of madmen. Beyond the bed is a bathroom. Jason pokes his head in and takes a quick survey of the room, then motions for me to pass.

The space is small, with a shower stall but no tub, a toilet and pedestal sink, and aqua blue tile lining the wall to shoulder height. There's a tiny frosted window that I studiously keep from glancing at.

Instead of leaving as I expect, he reaches past me and pushes aside the pale blue shower curtain. "You will clean yourself," he says. "I put your favorite shampoo and soap in here."

I don't know how to reply. This is simultaneously the most frightening and bizarre experience of my life. I'm afraid to do anything, afraid that it will be something that sets him off. "Thank you?" I try.

He continues to stand, watching me with an expectant expression in his eyes, and I realize he has no intention of leaving. "Jason, I can't use the bathroom with you standing there."

He shakes his head. "My sincere apologies, but I must stay. I have to make sure you cleanse well."

Cleansing? This guy was fruit loops. "But I need privacy for that."

With a sudden move that I fail to see coming, Jason casually backhands me, sending me careening with a cry into the porcelain pedestal sink and then falling against the toilet beside it. I scoot backwards, trying to make myself small enough to fit in the narrow gap between the toilet and the sink pedestal, but the cold porcelain stops me, biting into my back. I raise a hand that trembles to my cheek and bite my lip hard.

"Lesson two. There is no expectation of privacy when we are together. Lesson three. Do not talk back."

He moves to the side and turns the water in the shower on, testing the temperature with his hand. "Strip."

I eye him mutinously until he grows bored and makes a tsking sound with his teeth. "Honestly, darling, this feeble display is unworthy of you." Bending, he grabs a hunk of my hair and pulls me up. I grip his wrists and scream, but he holds me firmly with one hand and slaps me again with the other. This one catches me in the nose, and I feel it crunch, feel the blood spurt before I even see it drip on the white tile floor. Horrified, I raise my hands to my nose.

No one has ever hit me before. Not even a spanking as a child. I'm stunned by the casual brutality of Jason's action, and his ability to detach himself from them. It's like a separate part of him is instructing his movements. I can only stand, shaking, as he removes his knife and begins to cut my clothing off. He touches me as each new piece of skin is revealed, dragging the blade of the knife over the column of my throat and the slant of my shoulders, pressing the flat of the blade to my nipple. He's mumbling to himself as he makes his way down my body, ignoring my attempts to shrink away from the knife by holding me more firmly in place with the fingers still entwined in my hair.

When I'm nude, he shoves me roughly into the small shower cubicle. Cold water makes me flinch immediately "Wash," he instructs. "or I'll do it."

He leaves the shower curtain open, his eyes tracking me with a disturbed hunger as I soap my hands and begin to wash myself. I turn away from him, into the spray, and close my eyes. Ideas for escape, considered briefly and then discarded, tumble around inside my mind like shoes in a dryer. Instinct tells me that I'll have a single opportunity to make this work, so whatever I come up with needs to be impeccable as far as timing and planning. As much as his gaze makes my skin crawl at the moment, I have to shove my fear and disgust away for now.

Pretending that I'm not naked and shivering, I ask him the same thing I did earlier. He never gave me an answer. Not one that made sense, anyway. "Why me, Jason?"

From the corner of my eye I see him cross his arms over his chest and lean up against the sink. "I felt our connection from the very first time I saw you, Shiloh. You felt it, too. I could tell."

My eye throbs from his earlier backhand, and I can see the blood from my nose trickling sluggishly to the floor of the shower, running and mixing with the water. I phrase my response with care, not sure what will set him off or motivate another "lesson."

"You mean when we met at the hospital?" I'm finished showering, but afraid to turn the water off. Afraid of what happens next.

"No, Shiloh. Before that." His voice is calm, and inwardly I thank God I didn't trigger him. "You danced for me in the club before your brother ever became my patient. I felt our bond even through that glass partition. I knew instantly you were meant to be mine. And then you and Sammy appeared on my rounds…it was fate, Shiloh."

"What about Teddy?"

"What about him? I pick the girls; he just gets to play."

"G-girls?" My throat closes. "Are there others?" I force myself to look at him when he's silent. His face is stone.

"There have always been others," he finally answers.

"And what happened to the...others?" I'm shaking under the cold stream of water, but I'm not ready to move. Not ready to find out what happens next.

"We set them free."

Somehow, I don't think he has the same definition of the term that I do. "I...I don't know what to say." *Except may I have a towel, please.* The thought rises unbidden and I choke back hysterical laughter.

"Say you love me, like I asked you to weeks ago! Tell me you're mine!" He straightens and reaches past me, turning the water off with a hard twist. "Out." Grabbing the back of my neck, he half-pulls, half-pushes me out of the bathroom, shoving me to my knees when we cross the threshold into the bedroom. I cross my arms over my chest and hunch into myself, trying to shield my body from his eyes.

Teddy is in my peripheral, leaning against the jamb of the bedroom door. I hear a crunch, and realize he's eating an apple.

"Train her in the way," he murmurs to himself, eyes distant. I don't know what he means and don't want to ask. I clench my jaw, thinking of all the shifts I've worked with him at Kendrick's. All the times he fixed a drink for me or chatted over inconsequential nothings. I had started thinking of him as a trusted confidant.

"Teddy," I try. "Please help me. This isn't you."

He straightens from his lean. "You stupid whore. This is the real me. The Teddy at the bar? A façade. Just a layer."

Jason paces into my line of vision. "You're just like all the rest. Had to go and spread your legs for Mr. Popularity," he sneers. He paces in front of me as he spits the words, his agitation plain. "We couldn't just do this the easy way. You couldn't just accept that you were mine...had to go and fuck a student! Do you have any idea how much that hurt me, Shiloh? How humiliating it was for me?"

"I'm sorry, Jason. I'm so, so sorry—" The words are a sob. "Please—you're scaring me."

"I should've known you were a slut like all the others. After everything I did for you—"

"Please. I didn't know. I'm sorry."

He comes to a stop and thrusts his face inches away from mine. "You didn't know? How could you possibly not know, Shiloh?"

He's so close to me. And out of his freaking mind. Maybe I can take him off guard? Tentative, I reach out and place my hand on his shin as he looms over me. The khaki twill of his slacks is a strange reality in this twisted situation, but one I cling to. Literally. I curl my fingers into his pants and paint a pleading, sincere expression on my face as I lever myself up to my knees. "I know now," I say, and wrap my other arm around both of his legs, laying my cheek against the fabric covering his thigh. My skin crawls as his muscle jumps against my cheek. "I'm so sorry. Things will be different now that I know."

The room is silent save for his harsh breaths above me, and I try to gather courage to do what I need to do. As his hand descends, almost tender, on the top of my head, I gather my momentum and jerk his legs toward me and up as hard as I can.

It fucking works. Jubilation courses through me when his legs buckle and shoot out from under him. He crashes backward, head colliding with the dresser behind him, and I don't stay to see what happens next.

I run.

My dart for freedom is short-lived, though. I crash into Teddy's chest and he wraps his arms tightly around me. I kick and flail my lower body and feel him grunt, and then he flings us both onto the bed. I scream and fight like a banshee now, popping my neck up and trying to head butt him. I catch him in the mouth and feel blood drip down on me with satisfaction.

"Jason! Get the trap."

Jason groans from his position on the floor and I hear him moving. Teddy's using his weight to keep me pinned and has an arm across my throat, choking me...choking...The room darkens around the edges of my sight.

Stars dot my vision, and then they, too, fade to black.

28
Shiloh

I'M COLD.

There's utter, unbroken darkness around me, and a silence so deep it feels eternal.

I'm afraid to move or speak, afraid that I'm not alone and they're just waiting. Toying with me. I don't know which one I'm more afraid of. Separate, I think I could possibly get by Jason, although I may have ruined my chances earlier with that impulsive move. Teddy, though...Teddy is still waters. Despite working with him for so long, I don't know him well enough to predict his responses.

Hesitant, I clear my throat, and then wait. If they're here, they'll respond. Or I'll least hear a shift in breathing. Right?

Agonizing minutes stretch to eons and I hear nothing.

"Hello?" I whisper the word. The darkness absorbs the sound, abducts it and hides it, and I feel more alone than ever.

Finally, I stand.

I'm still naked, and everything feels sore and bruised. My shoulder, especially, radiates pain. It feels funny...disconnected. But my head is pounding, my nose thick and stuffy. I put a hand up to touch it and cry out.

It's the general soreness that bothers me, though, more than that. It's hard to pinpoint individual injuries. I'm sure some is from fighting against Teddy with every ounce of strength I had. There's a very female fear, though, that I can't dismiss. Did they rape me while I was unconscious?

Scared of the possibility, I nonetheless let my consciousness examine each sharp twinge and dull ache, reaching tentatively toward that place between my legs. I breathe a half-sob of relief when I'm satisfied that's the one spot on my body that isn't sore.

Now, my surroundings. I extend a hand against the darkness, searching. Feeling for something to give me some idea of where I am.

Anything.

This infinite darkness that surrounds me, coupled with the cold and a dank, musty smell, reminds me of a movie I watched once. It was a medieval tale, with an awful place called an oubliette used to hold prisoners.

It wasn't just any prison, though. Not just a dungeon or a place with bars. An oubliette was for those prisoners the captor wanted forgotten.

In all these weeks of being tormented by the specter of a stalker, I hadn't thought much about the *when*—the when I'd be taken. Such a scenario was an if, something to be wary of, to be prepared to defend myself against. It was a possibility, but one without form and shape.

I never allowed myself to acknowledge that possibility, to feed it the fuel of my fear and allow it to assume flesh and substance.

That was my first mistake.

My second: I'd clung to the why, and not the who.

I wish I'd pursued the *who* with more vigor. I wish I'd looked closer. Maybe then I wouldn't be here.

But what was that old saying? If wishes were horses, then beggars would ride.

My hand brushes stone. Further exploration of the divots that mar its surface and the presence of rounded seams makes me think cement cinder blocks. The floor beneath my feet is smooth and cold, transferring chill from its sub-surface. I can't reach the ceiling. When I try with both hands, my right shoulder gives a sharp pang and refuses to move. I'm in a basement of some sort.

"Okay, basement. Steps...there have to be steps." I murmur to myself. I need to hear my voice, hear something. This silence, this blackness...they're deafening.

I find a corner, and start examining the room with scientific precision. Two good strides take me to an opposite wall, another corner. So, around six feet. Two more strides to the next corner. The room is six by six. It's a concrete hole. I follow the perimeter, hands searching for a set of steps, or a ladder. When I reach the third corner, I back up a step and traverse the slight distance to the opposite wall. And then again. Pete and repeat.

There are no steps. There is no ladder.

No way out.

The realization hits me hard, a train barreling down the tracks of my awareness, and I sink to the floor. Pulling my knees to my chest, I rock, shoving down the screams that want to rise.

I rock, and I wait, craning my ears to hear the faintest sound from above me.

29
Gunner

THE DRIVE TO FIND SHILOH IS STEEPED IN SILENCE, save for the occasional comment coming through the Bluetooth from Twiggy, telling me to turn here or stay on the highway for a certain number of miles.

She's monitoring both Dr. Adams' cell signal and checking, in the background, on Brodie. I hear someone speaking after we've been driving a while, telling her they located Brodie near his bike in the lot across from Shiloh's house. He was unconscious, drugged, they think.

"Sheeit." I hear Shane mutter.

"Twig, do me a favor? Look up this other guy who didn't show up for work at Kendrick's. First name Teddy. Not sure of the last."

"Huh. Okay, give me a sec."

We can hear the clicking of her fingers on the keyboard. "You should be approaching a turn off, Gunner. On your right." A few seconds later, she continues. "K, club records say his name is Teddy Daniels..." More clicking. Then she stops, breath hitching in excitement. "Gunner. Daniels. Teddy—Theodore—Daniels. He's his brother!"

"Holy shit." Shane and I exchange looks.

"I never would have guessed that," Shane admits. "He seemed like a pretty decent dude." He drums his fingers on the armrest.

"I'm sure people thought that was the case with the good doctor, too."

"Take the next left, stay on that road for two miles. It'll take you straight to the destination," Twiggy breaks in. "G-Man, be careful. If they're both there..."

"Yeah, I know. Shane called the police when we left, but can you let them know the exact coordinates?"

"Way ahead of you."

"Any idea where they are?" Shane asks.

"They should be just a few minutes behind you. Both our detectives and the locals from that area."

I take the turn as Twiggy directs. We're deep in a section of woods on Claytor Mountain, which butts up against the back end of Thurston House. We had to drive around the world, it felt, to end up here, so I'm guessing that part of the facility's property is inaccessible by vehicle.

Or maybe Adams just wanted to drive in circles and disorientate his prisoner. I don't know.

After several yards I turn the headlights off, leaving only the muted gleam of the running lights to guide our way. As dark as it is, the headlights would act as a beacon of our arrival if anyone was watching. Shane lifts his chin at me in recognition.

"Stealth it is," he murmurs.

The road, a narrow single lane, soon becomes a rutted gravel track. We follow it carefully until I spot a flash of light ahead, and then I pull to the side of the road and cut the engine. "We need to walk in from here," I tell Shane, and we both climb out.

We follow the gravel track toward the light, which flickers in and out of tree branches. The road opens up into a gravel drive, circling around in front of a tiny cabin. Two cars are parked in front. I dip inside the tree line, Shane at my back, and we watch for a moment.

Shadows behind the curtains move back and forth at the window, indistinct. It's quiet, with only the distant yip of a coyote breaking the hush. Either no one's making any sound inside, or we simply can't hear at this distance. "Let's see if there are multiple entrances," I tell Shane, starting to rise. He halts me with a hand on my arm.

"I'll go. You stay, watch. If there's another way in, I'll text you my location and we can go in at the same time." I nod and he's off, sprinting across the scrabbly yard with his hoody pulled up over his head.

A minute later, my cell buzzes with a notification. There's a back entrance. I make my way to the front door. "Ready?" I text Shane, and he replies with a thumbs up. "On three, then." I send the next text, give him a second for read time, and then count under my breath.

"—three."

The door gives way easily against my shoulder, and in a back corner of the small structure I hear Shane doing the same. My attention, though, is focused on the two men before me. Teddy had been laying on the couch, but the door's inward crash makes him jump up in surprise. Adams stops in the act of pacing.

"Where is she?"

Adams flicks a quick look over his shoulder at his brother, who rises to stand beside him. Teddy, leaner and slighter than Adams, turns to look behind them at Shane, standing in a doorway behind them. He shakes his head slightly in response to my arched brow.

"You're too late," he answers, hands coming up in a defensive stance.

I feel the roar building inside me with his words and launch myself across the room at him. From the corner of my eye I see Shane doing the same with the bartender.

Adams and I clash in the center of the room, arms grappling and bodies circling until I finally kick a foot out and manage to sweep him to the floor. I follow, straddling him and descending into a punch to the jaw that makes my knuckles ache and his head whip to the side. I feel my lips twist in mirthless humor. He's a big fucker but he can't take a punch. He's out in only two more punches, face bloodied but not battered enough for my approval. That was far too easy. I want to keep hitting, and so I do, fists landing with the sound of satisfaction against his flesh.

"Gunner." Shane's hands come under my arms, haul me back. "Gunner, you need to stop. You hear that?"

Dimly, I can hear sirens.

I look around and see Teddy lying prone on the floor.

"He said we were too late." My eyes move frantically to Shane's and I fist his shirt in both hands. "Where is she? Where the fuck did they put her?"

"We'll find her, man."

Shane's reassurance goes unanswered as police begin to stream through the open door. After we identify ourselves, they make short work of cuffing Adams and Teddy, pulling them out of the house and placing them in the backs of two separate cruisers.

We answer questions from a couple of detectives for what seems like hours but is probably only minutes, while several cops move quickly throughout the cabin, searching.

"Someone get me the county specs on this place," a detective calls out.

The answer floats in from the yard. "On it."

I sink down on a faded sofa that looks like it came

straight from the seventies, leaning into my elbows on my knees. Voices blur in the background and I struggle to curb the adrenaline still coursing through my body and urging me to move. Do something. Find her.

I have to find her. I don't want to consider another scenario. I can't think about any alternative option.

Don't want to imagine a world without Shiloh in it.

I take in a breath, breathe it out hard through my nose. Everyone pauses at the sound, and in the silence that ensues I hear a faint cry.

One of the detectives starts to talk and is abruptly shushed. No one moves. "Shiloh?" I speak her name into the expectant air, and then yell it, jumping up. "Shiloh! Baby, answer me!"

We wait, and in a moment are gifted with a second cry. "Below us!" Shane calls, and starts kicking the rug back. "She's below us—"

As the rug is peeled back, the lines of a trap door in the floor come into view. I'm scrabbling at them before the ring to pull it open is even revealed, and then yanking that up so fiercely I almost pull it from its cleverly concealed hinges. And there she is, standing below us in the light that filters down through the square and looking up, arms crossed over her bare breasts. "Somebody get me a blanket," I command, and look around for a way to get down there to her. There's some kind of mechanism just inside the frame. I tug at it and a set of ladder-like steps begins to slowly descend. Shiloh is openly weeping. *OhGodohGodohGod, please let her be okay.*

I don't realize I'm chanting the words out loud until I feel Shane's hand on my shoulder, squeezing hard.

The stairs are three-quarters of the way down, Shiloh already reaching for them. "Hold on, baby. Hang on." I start to descend, and someone tosses a blanket down after me. Halfway down I jump down, clutching Shiloh and the blanket she's already started wrapping around herself to me in a hold so tight I have to remind myself to be gentle.

I pull back, running my hands over her roughly. "Are you hurt, sweetheart? Did either of those fuckers put their hands on you?" I keep my voice low. "Am I going to hurt you when I pick you up?"

"I'm okay. He hit me...I think threw me down here when I passed out. Something's wrong with my shoulder."

Her voice is a hoarse rasp.

"Choked you?" My hands trace the bruising on her throat, and she nods. "Come on, *dolcezza*." I manage to wrap her around me and ascend the steps.

A paramedic waits at the top. "We have a bus out here," he says. I follow along behind and a female paramedic helps me lay her on a gurney, preserving her modesty as she does. They stop me as I'm climbing in alongside Shiloh, her hand clutching mine.

"Only family, sir."

"But—" Shiloh whispers.

"I'm all she has here," I tell them. "I'm her family."

The female paramedic hesitates, then jerks her head. "Don't get in the way."

"I'm right here," I tell Shiloh, fastening my eyes to hers as I sit beside her. "I'm not leaving you. Not ever again."

30
Shiloh

It's the dream that wakes me.

It's dark and I'm cold, and there's a faint sound from across the room. Or maybe it's above me. I can't tell.

I can't breathe, either, a pressure on my throat cutting off my oxygen. Then I'm falling. I brace for landing, feeling it before it comes in every muscle of my body. I just keep falling, though.

I hear voices, and I try to shout, to make myself heard.

No one's listening, though. No one hears.

Then a door opens, and a pocket of light appears, a male form leaning over the opening, blocking the light. Only...it's not Gunner. It's them, one man blurring into two, and suddenly I realize I still can't breathe—

With a gasp I sit upright, hands to my throat. He's there in an instant, hands on my cheeks turning my head firmly to look at him, indistinct words falling from his lips. It takes me a second, but it registers, the pressure on my throat dissipating.

It's Gunner's face in my sight. Gunner's hands hauling me roughly up against him. Gunner's arms wrapping me close and holding me tightly on his lap.

Gunner.

"You're okay. You're safe. I'm here."

I'm in the hospital. I remember arriving, being hooked up to an IV, a doctor setting my nose and fixing my shoulder, which had been dislocated. I'm pretty sure he gave me a sedative before doing all that, because I half-floated through it and then fell asleep.

Now, the light above the sink is on, but the rest are off, casting the room into shadow. The room is clear of people, except Gunner.

"I was dreaming," I tell him now.

He settles himself more comfortably on the bed, raising the back until he's half-sitting, half-reclining. One big hand comes to rest on my hair, and he gently presses my head into his chest. "You want to talk about it?"

"No." I answer quickly, and feel his arms tighten around me. "I'm just so glad you found me."

"It was Cotton, texting Shane. And Twiggy, tracking the cell signal."

"And you, not quitting."

"Never, baby."

"You're calling me baby a lot. What happened to *dolcezza*?"

His shoulder shrugs beneath me and I feel his lips against my hair. "You're still my *dolcezza*. You're just baby, too. And you need to sleep."

"I don't think I can. There's this part of me that doesn't believe it's over. I don't know how to be…normal…anymore."

"Well, it is over. They're locked up. Shiloh…Jason Adams is singing like a bird. He's confessed to the two of them being involved with that girl missing from the University of Virginia. They're searching for her, too. Her body."

I flinch, pity moving through me for the one that came before me. Gunner sees and tightens his arms around me. "More, there are others. They won't be getting out in this lifetime."

I shudder. "Stay with me?"

He kisses my hair again. "You don't need to ask."

I fall asleep, secure in his arms and comforted by the knowledge that he'll be there when I wake.

But when morning comes, he's gone.

TWIGGY COMES TO PICK ME UP.

She knocks hesitantly on the partially open door, her colorful striped beanie preceding her as she peeks in, as if she half expects me to throw her out.

"Come in, Twiggy." I don't have the energy to be angry. I look at her dully and she enters all the way, coming to stand beside the bed.

She places a bag on the end and sits in the chair next to me. "Hey."

It's rude, but I can't even bring myself to reply. I know why she's here. Gunner sent her. He said he wouldn't leave, but he did, and he isn't coming back to pick me up himself. I close my eyes, hoping the liquid that pools in the corners goes unnoticed.

"Gunner sent me," she confirms. "I brought some clothes for you to change into, your phone—all fixed, by the way." She digs the phone with its shiny, uncracked screen out of the bag and I take it, looking quickly to see if he messaged me.

No.

"Thank you," I manage. "The nurse said I could leave as soon as someone was here to pick me up."

"And here I am!" she says brightly.

Climbing cautiously from the bed so I don't jostle my shoulder, I turn my back to her and start to get dressed. She can see every bruise and laceration on me, but I don't care.

It doesn't matter.

"He wanted to come, Shiloh." Her voice behind me is soft, sympathetic.

"It's whatever." I finish dressing and ball the bag up to toss. I arrived here last night with nothing; I'm leaving with nothing. "I'm ready."

She doesn't rise to follow me until I'm out the door, looking uncertainly down the hall. I'm not sure which direction to take. "Left." She steers me in the right direction. "He's not handling this whole thing very well."

I snort. "It's okay, Twiggy. I deserve it."

"No—sheesh, he knew this is what you'd think. This has nothing to do with your five-minute break-up. He's not abandoning you."

"Then what the hell is it?"

"He didn't state anything explicitly. You know how dudes are. All I know is that he climbed on that motorcycle and said he needed some air."

I think about this while we ride the elevator to the parking garage. I can't think of any other reason for Gunner to have left other than my Dear John letter.

Twiggy points the way to her vehicle, a vintage-looking muscle car that she calls a Hellcat. It suits her, spunky and classy with a side of kiss my ass. I climb in and sink down into the leather seats, gingerly pulling my seatbelt across my lap.

"Look...I appreciate your defense of Gunner. And I thank you—so, so much—for your part in getting me out of that cabin last night." She waves her hand to dismiss the idea and I ignore her. "I will always be grateful. But I can't talk about this right now."

"I get it. And I'll shut up."

I relax into the seat with a sigh as she pulls out of the parking garage.

"After I say this one thing. That man was an absolute mess over you. I mean, technically he's kind of always been, ever since that party five years ago. But when you went missing...Shiloh, I've never seen him like this. He held it together, but by a hair."

"I've never doubted his feelings for me, Twiggy. I hate that he went through that."

We're quiet for the remainder of the drive home, Twiggy appearing to have said her piece and me in no mood to talk. When she pulls in the driveway, though, she speaks again.

"I just thought you should know. He was trying so hard to keep his head on straight so he could find you...I don't think he had time to process everything, you know? All the might have beens, the coulda-shoulda-woulda's...the what-ifs. He didn't consider those while we were looking. And afterwards, it just hit him."

I nod. "I understand."

Twiggy is growing frustrated. "No, Shiloh—I don't think you do. He was on the phone with me when he left your hospital room early this morning. He had to set the phone down so he could puke." I press my lips firmly together to keep myself from crying. "So just don't be too hard on him when he comes around. 'Cause he'll be back."

Late that night, I send Gunner a message.

Me: I don't know where you are. I just want to say…

I break off. There's so much I want to say. *I love you. Thank you for saving my life. Don't leave me.*

In the end, I tell him simply *thank you*.

"IT'S OVER. IT'S ALL OVER, COTTON."

"Oh, thank God." Cotton drops her head into her hands, the stifled sounds of her weeping coming to me clearly from wherever it is she's stationed. "I'm so sorry you had to go through that, Shiloh. So fucking sorry. If I had just told Shane to call the police immediately—"

"It wouldn't have made a difference. I was gone almost as soon as he got here."

"If I had just called out, then, when we were on Skype. Maybe if he saw he had a witness he wouldn't have taken you."

"We can't play the what-if game, Cotton. If he hadn't taken me then, it would have been another time. Bottom line is you saved my life by listening to your instincts and messaging Shane when you did."

I was still reeling from everything I'd learned following the day of my abduction. In the days that followed, I learned that Gunner and Shane had found me through Cotton. I owed Shane, and I was going to have to come to terms with my attitude towards him. I'd been wrong about him and he deserved an apology. I learned that Twiggy discovered Brodie, drugged and unconscious beside his bike down the street from my house.

Twiggy and Detective Morris told me how they'd figured out that both Jason Adams and Teddy Daniels were the adopted sons of Beatrice Thurston. Although as different as night and day on the surface, years of emotional and physical abuse at the hands of Beatrice had warped them both, giving them a skewed perspective of and hatred for women.

After Jason Adams had confessed to multiple abductions and murders with his brother, a search of the mountain near Thurston House revealed that I was not the first woman they had obsessed over and stalked. The police discovered four graves on the property, and Detective Morris confirmed that the bodies of three missing women had been identified. One was the brothers' adopted mother, Beatrice. The police were uncertain if she had died of natural causes, as she was nearing the end stage of stage four lung cancer, or if one or both brothers had sped up the process.

Although still pending dental examination, detectives were certain that the second grave belonged to

Teddy's high school girlfriend, who had gone missing almost a decade earlier. Evidence with the body—an inscribed necklace—led them to conjecture as much.

The third grave belonged to a woman who had been reported missing a year earlier. The fourth, to Madison Bryan, the student who had recently disappeared from a college campus around an hour away.

It chilled my blood to think I could have filled a fifth grave. But it was over now.

"Stop that," I tell Cotton. "You're going to get me going and I am sick to death of crying."

Cotton wipes her eyes. "I know, I'm sorry. I just want to be there. Just want to wrap you in a big old hug and put you in my pocket."

"You can do that when you get home—the hug part, anyway. Just a few months, right? You'll be home by the end of the school year?"

"Unless they extend this deployment, yeah."

"They'd better not. And how long will you be here for?"

Cotton squirms in her seat and excitement lights her eyes. "Well, that's what I was going to tell you the other day when we were so rudely interrupted. I committed to four years active duty and four inactive. I'll be on inactive duty when I come home, for all intents and purposes a civilian. I'll be home to stay, unless they call me back to active duty."

"Oh, my God, Cotton—I have no words! That's amazing. Do you have any idea what you want to do when you get here?"

"Sleep?" Cotton chuckles. "Not entirely. I'm sure I'll be job hunting for a while."

I smirk at her. "I hear there's an opening at Kendrick's."

"Ha, ha. Maybe I'll apply to teach at the high school and snag me a hot senior. Speaking of, what's up with you and Gunner?"

I feel my body tense. "Absolutely nothing."

"What?"

"I'm serious. He rode with me in the ambulance, sat with me the entire time I was in the hospital, said he wouldn't leave. Then I woke the next morning and he was gone. Twiggy brought me home and I haven't heard from him since."

"Well, what happened?"

I shake my head. "That's just it. I don't know. He was calling me baby. Holding me. I don't understand why he would just…leave. Not even call."

"Have you tried calling him?"

I shift uneasily. "I sent him a text."

"You sent him a text." Her voice is flat.

"Cotton…you don't understand."

"I understand you're a wuss. Shy, the guy hauled ass to freaking rescue you, and you send him a text? You need to get over there and give him a blow job."

Despite myself, I laugh. "I'm terrified, Cotton. What if this is his way of telling me he doesn't want me anymore?"

"That was the risk you took, right? If that's the case, you suck it up. Now. I gotta go. You, my friend—pull up your big girl panties and go. Grovel."

I swallow around the lump in my throat. "You always did shoot straight. Okay. Going to grovel."

"Do not pass go, do not collect two hundred dollars. Put some shoes on your feet and move your ass, soldier."

I give her a salute. "Love you, babe."

"Love you back. Let me know how it goes."

"I will." I kiss my fingers and touch them briefly to the screen, watching as Cotton does the same. And then it's just me, sitting in my quiet, empty house.

It has never felt as empty as it does without Gunner. In the short amount of time we were together, he filled the small space, every corner, with his larger-than-life presence. Sitting here in the living room, the Christmas tree reminds me of his patience in fluffing the branches. His arms around me as we laid on the floor and watched the blinking lights.

The lights are off now, the tree a dull, dark green without their illumination, even as the room bright with sunshine streaming through the new window that someone had arranged to have replaced yesterday. I move to the tree and click the lights on.

I can do this. I have to do this. The thought galvanizes me, spurs me to action. I drag my furry sheepskin boots over my bare feet. My legs, still in my sleep shorts, are bare, but I don't want to waste time finding clothes. I yank on a sweatshirt that's laying on the couch and grab up my purse from the coffee table.

My hand is inches from the doorknob when I stop. Nerves stunt my will. What if he shuts me down? What if he doesn't love me anymore? I feel my heart crack a little at the idea. He said we weren't done in the library, but what if he really is exactly that—done? Maybe it would be better to wonder, than to know for sure.

When the hell did he become so important to me? I bow my head, releasing an unsteady breath. I can't lose him. Not him, too.

My earlier words to Cotton return to me as I stand there, indecision a paralytic. *We can't play the what-if game.*

I steel myself. Open the door.

And there he is.

31
Gunner

HAND POISED TO KNOCK ON SHILOH'S DOOR, I just barely catch myself when it swings open to reveal her standing on the threshold.

"Gunner." Her eyes go wide, and I move the fist I have raised, raking it instead through my hair. I'm nervous. Why the hell am I nervous?

"Shiloh. May I come in?"

"Of course." Shiloh steps back, giving me space to enter, and I move past her into the living room, trying to ignore the instant flare of heat as our bodies brush.

"Did I interrupt something? It looked like you were on your way outside." I shove my hands in my pockets and wait as Shiloh closes the door and comes to stand before me, her arms crossed over her chest.

"I was leaving to find you, actually." Her toe, clad in a ridiculous looking furry boot, draws a pattern on the carpet.

I arch a brow at her outfit. "In your pajamas?"

She reddens. "I was in a hurry." After a beat, she adds, "I didn't want to give myself time to change my mind."

I blow out a breath. She's nervous, too. "Sit down, Shy." I wait for her to seat herself on the sofa and then lower myself to sit beside her, steepling my fingers in front of me as I observe her without speaking. Her left cheek boasts mottled purple and red bruising that extends to her eye and brow where that monster hit her, and a small white bandage crosses the bridge of her nose where he broke it. Reaching out a finger, I touch it lightly with a grimace. "We're a matched pair." The thick silence resumes.

"Gunner—"

"Shiloh—"

We speak at the same time and fall quiet once again. I gesture with my hand. "Ladies first."

"Okay." She takes in a deep breath. "I was on my way to see you because I wanted to thank you. Properly. Not in a text message."

"Jesus, Shiloh, you don't need to fucking thank me."

She holds up a hand. "I'm sorry about that. Sending a text message, I mean, instead of just calling you." She shakes her head, her hair falling in a messy curtain around her face. "But you left me. You said you'd stay, and when I woke up, you were gone, and I...I don't know what I was thinking." She pauses, tilts her head. "That's not true. I was thinking, *damn, this is scary.* I was scared, Gunner. I'm still scared—"

"What were you scared of, Shy?" I'm having a hard time catching her eye. Her gaze is darting everywhere, refusing to land on any one thing. I cup her cheeks in my hands, angling her face so she stills. "Look at me." Her bottom lip trembles before she catches it and presses them tight together. "I'm sorry I'm left. It didn't have anything to do with you, though. I would never hurt you, Shy. You know that."

She starts to speak and I stop her. "I didn't want to scare you or make you feel badly, and I needed...there was all this anger building inside me. It was a physical thing. I had to let it out." I let out a chuckle devoid of humor. "As soon as I stepped outside the hospital I puked my guts up."

"Twiggy told me."

"Then I went home, got drunk, hit the bag—"

"Hit the bag?"

"We have a heavy bag in the gym." She nods. "Drank some more...I'm sorry, baby. It just took me a minute to get my head straight." I dip my face down to hers and kiss her, my lips brushing lightly against hers once, twice.

"I was scared you might break my heart," she whispers, so low I have to strain to hear her, even as close as we are. "And the hell of it is, I'd deserve it. You have the power to hurt me more than anyone or anything else, Gunner. I'm so glad you just had to puke and get drunk."

She catches me off guard and I let out a short laugh. I'd come here anticipating her being mad as hell and expecting I'd have to fight to get us back to where we were, and honestly, I was tired of fighting. Tired of not being sure of her. Of us. Not that it'd make me stop fighting, but still.

She's blown the fight clean off course, though. Laid herself bare in front of me. "I'm not going to break your heart, Shy," I say, staring hard into her eyes. "As long as you stop breaking mine. Deal?"

She nods, crumpling against my chest. I can feel the shuddering breath she releases as I lower my hands and pull her onto my lap, winding my arms around her. "I love you, Shiloh. I loved you yesterday, love you today, and want to love you for the rest of your tomorrows. I want to be with you and want you to be with me. Is that good enough?"

"Yes." The word is a sob. "I love you, too. I was so scared I'd fucked up. That you were just done."

"Never, *dolcezza*." Tipping her chin up, I press my lips to hers, knowing I've finally reclaimed the heaven I discovered long ago, once upon a closet.

Epilogue
Shiloh

"Do I really have to do this?"

"Yes! Get in there." Esme shoves me into the closet—the same one I visited with Gunner not too long ago—and shuts the door. Her footsteps recede down the hallway and I realize she's not going to turn the light on for me. Why is the switch on the outside of the closet, anyway?

It's not pitch black. Light seeps from the crack at the bottom of the door, and its seams are limned with the brightness beyond.

But still. I don't like the dark, not after my experience. Even today, as we celebrate Christmas Eve together weeks later, it's too fresh. I can feel my anxiety building, a sense of panic bubbling just under the surface. My imagination runs away with me, and I fancy I can hear someone in here with me. Breathing.

Screw this. Opening the door a few inches, I slide my hand out and feel around on the wall outside the closet for the switch plate. "Eureka." I find it, my hand closing over and flipping the small switch, and light, blessed light floods the small room. With a sigh of relief, I close the door and look around for a spot to sit down while I wait.

The closet has acquired new tenants since I last visited, months ago when Gunner kissed me silly. When we were here then, it was home to sporting supplies and winter coats. Now, there are several cardboard boxes stacked along the bottom, and a hip-height cage that looks like a dog kennel.

Huh. Maybe Esme is getting a dog for Christmas? I've always felt they needed one around here.

After testing the sturdiness of the cage, I perch on its edge and inspect my fingernails as I wait. They need work. My hands and nails are chapped and dry, probably from being outside. I've been spending a lot of time here with Gunner, just walking the vineyard and reacquainting myself with my camera. My hands reflect the cold, dry wind that's been a constant the past several weeks.

New year's resolution: lotion up.

The door opens then, interrupting my inspection. I look up and instantly feel my heart swell. "Sammy?" I stand and just barely manage to keep from flinging myself at him. He's standing…walking…on his own. He's here. "You're here?" I breathe.

He grins and wraps me in a hug. "Surprise."

"I don't understand." Behind him, Gunner and his family stand, beaming. "They said January."

I'd been busy with plans for Sammy's homecoming next month, moving furniture and giving the house a thorough cleaning. He'd remained at Thurston House even after Dr. Adams' arrest, just under a different doctor's care. The board had been swift in disassociating itself from the former physician, ensuring that no whiff of scandal touched their facility. Sammy agonized over the fact that it was his doctor who had been stalking me, feeling like indirectly he was at fault.

I understood feeling responsible. It would take time, I thought, for both of us to get past that. Ironically,

Sammy's sense of guilt was helping me see the futility of my own and understand how misplaced it was.

Now, Sammy's cheeks tinge pink. "I might have asked them to mislead you a little," he admits.

"You...!" I slap his chest playfully. "And you." Releasing Sammy, I go to Gunner and wrap my arms around his waist, lifting my face for him to drop a light kiss on my lips. "I can't believe you kept this a secret."

He grunts. "Yeah, well, it wasn't easy. You were always around. He's actually been here a week already."

"Here? Really? How did I miss this?"

"Gunner kept you busy," Esme snarks. "Twiggy and I kept Sam company."

"This is the best gift ever. Thank you." I kiss Gunner once again, then release him. "I guess now we just need to get things moving at the house!"

"Yeah, well, wanted to talk to you about that, actually. Sam's not supposed to be on his own for a few more months, until he's one hundred percent released. He's doing great here, and we already have the gym, the pool, everything he needs. I thought maybe we could take our time, finish fixing up your house so it's perfect when he's ready to be on his own."

I nod. "That sounds fine. Great, really. I'm kind of glad I don't have to buy a lot of fancy equipment."

The others start making their way down the hall. "We'll be in the great room," Mike calls.

"That's not all." Gunner waits until my attention returns to him. "I was kind of hoping you would stay."

I'm confused. "I'm already kind of staying, Gunner. And of course, I'd stay, take care of anything Sammy needs—"

"No, that's not what I'm talking about. I want you to *stay*, stay. Stay with me. Be with me."

"Live with you?"

"I want more than just a few nights when our schedules are clear. I want you here when I go to bed. Here when I wake up. I want you surrounded by my family. One day, I want to surround you with our family." He started off hesitantly, but he's picking up steam as he continues, his hands taking hold of my upper arms. "I know it's soon. I know we're young. Both of us, not just me. I also know that this—" He gestures between us. "Us...we're right. We don't have to get married right away, but I want us to be together. Committed, me to you, and you to me. I—"

"Yes."

He stops and stares. Moves his hands to my neck, thumbs grazing the skin of my jaw with tenderness. "Yes?"

I nod within his grasp. My arms twine around him of their own volition, snaking their way around his waist to hold him to me. "Yes. As long as we have our own space."

He's right. It's crazy. It is too soon and we— especially him—are young. But it's true, what he said. *We're right.*

We were right when he was ten and I was thirteen and he was my annoying little brother's best friend. We were right a few years later, when he made my toes curl with a kiss that was more feeling than skill. And we're right, now, despite everything common sense and society dictates.

It's only been a few months since Gunner walked into my classroom, but it feels like we've lived entire lifetimes since then, only to circle back to where we first began: with a closet.

With a kiss.

Gunner dips his head and kisses me, and just like the first time, I'm lost to the thrill of his lips against mine. I feel that kiss on my lips, but also in the coiling deep in my belly and the zip of electricity down my spine. He moves his hands from my jaw to the back of my head, tangling in my hair, and I sigh into his mouth. He devours it, that sigh, and seeks for more.

It's sweet and sensual, our lips moving together like they have a dozen other times. This kiss is different though. It's a promise, an avowal. It tells me without words that I'm his, and there's nothing he wants more—not sex, not air, not water in the desert—not anything more than me, right here, with his mouth on mine and his hands in my hair. Just me.

And I return the sentiment, believing fully in that promise of him and me, together.

Something edges into my awareness with a sharp yip of sound. I break away and stare dazedly up at Gunner.

"What was that?"

"What was what?"

His expression is bland, and I look at him closely. "Really? You didn't hear that—" The sound comes again and I cock my head. "There! Did someone get a dog?"

"I have no idea...let's go see."

As we emerge from the doorway to the closet and head down the hall, I hear a muffled exclamation and a thud, and then the unmistakable sound of nails clicking on hardwood floors.

Canine nails.

Gunner's eyes meet mine and he can't hide the gleam that makes them sparkle like diamonds, or the wide grin that flashes his dimples.

"What have you done?"

He shrugs in reply, just as the click of nails becomes the full-fledged slide of a puppy darting around the corner.

I drop to my knees. "Oh. My. God! You are just the cutest wittle thing ever in the whole wide world." My voice ascends immediately into high-pitched baby talk as I grab the wriggling yellow beast and hold it out for a good look.

She is a tiny monster. All spit and squirm and golden fur with tiny brown splotches—like freckles—and hound dog ears. "What is she? She's so cute! Is she Esme's? Oh, Gunner, I need this dog!" I wail the last sentence, never for a moment thinking she's actually mine, until Gunner squats beside me and plucks at dangling silver icon on her collar.

"She's yours, baby. Read her collar." He laughs as the dog licks his hand and twists to get free. Gunner helps me hold her still and I lift the heart-shaped pendant. *Goldie. If found, please call…* and a phone number.

"You can change her name if you want. She's a type of hound dog, a leopard. They're highly intelligent and affectionate. And energetic. I thought she'd be good when you're walking around, taking your pictures. And if you don't like her—"

Gunner rattles on, but I'm caught in the puppy's limpid brown gaze. She's chewing on my shirt and peeking up at me, as if to ask, *is this okay?*

More than okay. I smile and rub behind her ears.

"She's perfect, Gunner." I press a kiss to his jawline, nuzzling until my mouth is next to his ear. "I might even think about getting up with her at night."

"Are y'all going to sit around and smooch all day or are we going to eat? Kiss the girl and c'mon." Esme shakes her head and disappears around the corner, the sounds of her footsteps announcing her path toward the formal dining area.

Gunner pulls me to my feet, lifting the puppy as we go. "We'd better go. The natives are restless."

With one final kiss and hands firmly, unashamedly linked, we make our way down the hall to our family.

THE END

ABOUT THE AUTHOR

Elle Rae Whyte is a simple girl at heart, living life on a farm in the foothills of the Blue Ridge Mountains. She has three kids, four if you count the husband, and numerous fur babies that like to cuddle while she's writing.

Follow the author for upcoming release information.

BookBub: https://bit.ly/2ZPXL7i
Newsletter: https://bit.ly/31Mr0Jq
Facebook: https://bit.ly/3eZd1nP
Instagram: https://bit.ly/2OMUzUW
Twitter: https://bit.ly/32PtAR2
Amazon: https://amzn.to/3gXRSw8
Goodreads: https://bit.ly/37voiKN

Printed in Great Britain
by Amazon

56322555R00154